AN *ALPHACHAT.COM* NOVEL

VICTORIA ASHLEY & HILARY STORM

Pay for Play
Copyright © 2016 Victoria Ashley & Hilary Storm

All rights reserved. Without limiting the rights under copyright reserved above, no part of this publication may be reproduced, stored in or introduced into a retrieval system, or transmitted, in any form, or by any means such as electronic, mechanical, photocopying, recording, or otherwise without the prior written permission of the author of this book. This is a work of fiction. Names, characters, places, brands, media, and incidents are either the product of the author's imagination or are used fictitiously. The author acknowledges the trademarked status and trademark owners of various products referenced in this work of fiction, which have been used without permission. The publication/use of these trademarks is not authorized, associated with, or sponsored by the trademark owners.

Cover model:
Darren Birks

Photographer:
Darren Birks Photography

Cover Designer:
Dana Leah, Designs by Dana

Editor:
Kellie Montgomery

Interior Design & Formatting by:
Christine Borgford, Perfectly Publishable

Chapter ONE

Rebel

WHAT THE HELL IS THIS crap . . . I hold the packet up as I flip through the crisp white pages one last time, trying to wrap my head around everything that this process entails. Was the person who created this application completely drunk and out of their mind? Seriously; I want to know.

All this just for a job at *Club Royal*. This was not what I was expecting when I walked through those overly expensive gold and pearl doors a few hours ago seeking information. I know it's an exclusive club, but this is just beyond crazy. The club has a street named just for it. Of course they're going to expect too much.

Sitting back in my chair, I let out a tired laugh and shake my head, trying to make sure that I'm seeing correctly.

One year contract.
Exclusive to Club Royal.
On call every weekend.
No drinking during shift.
No dating any other employees of Royal Inc.
Boyfriend/girlfriend not allowed at club during shift.

Keep the drama at home.
Performance evaluation done by management once a month.
No drugs.

That's not even all the rules. This is only from the first page. There's at least two more pages of regulations left to go and six pages of who knows what.

I jump in my seat when my roommate slams the front door closed and starts yelling. "Go away, asshole!"

Remi turns back to the door when her "friend" Taylor drunkenly mumbles something from the other side. "Just go home and go to bed, Taylor. You're getting on my damn nerves tonight."

She walks away from the door, plops down on the couch and turns on the TV as if she wasn't just making a scene at the door a few seconds ago. "What's for dinner?" She leans over the back of the couch to look at me. "I'm starving and I've wasted my last bit of energy arguing with that jerkoff."

Holding up the papers, I roll my eyes and toss them to her. "I haven't had a chance to eat. I've been looking for a side job to give me a break from the monotonous computer work I do." I walk over to the couch and hover over her shoulder. "I've been trying to wrap my head around this stupid application for *Club Royal*. Is the owner nuts or what?"

I close my eyes and try to get an image of what the owner must look like as Remi fingers through all of the information.

"I'm guessing the owner is some short, bald man with a tiny penis. I wouldn't be surprised if his belly hangs over his belt and he has overly small feet, yet he wants his employees to be top notch," I mutter. "I'm not sure a second job is worth all that, Remi. I'll just stick to webpage design for now."

"Good choice." She tosses the packet down onto the coffee table in front of her, before giving me an odd look and watching me walk back over my desk to take a seat.

"What?" I tiredly blow my hair out of my face. I've spent the last ten damn hours behind this computer and I can barely stand to look at it for another second. "Are you going to tell me how I look like shit again, because trust me, I know. No need to hear it from you. I'm exhausted and my eyes hurt like hell."

She smiles, flashing me her perfect pearly whites. "I was just thinking . . ." Her eyebrows raise, concerning me. It's never good when she thinks. "You're in front of that screen all day, like you said, and I feel like you need a damn good reason to *love* that computer again so you won't need a break. You need to want to make love to it, baby."

"Should I be scared?" I ask.

"Not if you like beautiful dicks."

I was just taking a drink of my water, while finishing up a new design and her words cause me to spit all over the screen and everything around it.

"Does that mean you don't like beautiful dicks . . . or that you do?" I watch her as she stands up and walks to the kitchen. "There's this website called Alphachat.com." She pulls out two glasses of wine and taps one of the stools, for me to take a seat next to her. "And oh my god, I swear with *everything* in me that the top Alpha of that shit has the prettiest dick I've ever laid eyes on. What I wouldn't give to run my tongue over the head of it."

I grab for the glass of wine as she holds it out for me. "What the fuck? Is that what you do on your days off when you lock yourself in your room all day and I'm stuck cleaning by myself?"

She shrugs. "Yeah. It's a very good reason too, so don't give me that look. I work hard during the week and I deserve to unwind and trust me . . . Taylor was not doing the job. This pussy needs a real man to get off and these men are top notch Alpha males that know how to touch themselves so good that I even got off without touching myself once. That's some heaven right there, Honey."

She tilts her head back and laughs, causing her brown curls to bounce over her shoulders. "You need to loosen up some. A whole lot, actually."

"Yeah," I whisper while tiredly swirling my wine glass. "I suppose I do, but to watch some stranger touch himself? That seems kind of dirty if you ask me."

"Dirty is the best way to go, my friend. That's exactly why I made you an account and added you to Mr. Lynx Kade's waiting list. You're welcome."

"You did what?" I ask in a panic.

"Don't worry," she laughs. "I didn't use your real name and there's a private button you can hit so they can hear you but not see you. It will probably be weeks before you get in Lynx's private room, but you should really take Blaze, Knox or Nash for a ride first to warm you up. Any of the boys are good. Time to dust the cobwebs off your vagina and put it to use again after what seven . . . eight months of no action." She lifts a concerned brow.

"Actually, *six*." I grunt when she smiles in amusement. "You find this funny, huh? Well trust me, my vagina has been fine without some lying, cheating asshole around to think he's entitled to have his way with it whenever he wants."

"Yeah well with the Alpha boys, there's no touching or having their way with you required. I left a sticky note with the website info along with your username and password on the side of the monitor in case you want to be nice to your vagina for once." She stands up and walks back to the fridge, opening it again. "I'm gonna grab the leftovers from last night and just retire to my room to watch old Jason Statham movies. God, that man is sexy." She turns to me and holds up the bag of Chinese from last night.

"You want any before I spread it out all over my bed and have my way with it?" She winks.

Laughing, I shake my head and set my wine glass down. "No. It's all yours."

"Cool." She stops at her doorway and turns back to face me. "Just do yourself a favor and check out the website. You work really hard and if anyone deserves a man to do *whatever* he's told for once, it's you. You enter that private room and those boys will do anything and everything you tell them to. Sometimes they try to get you to give them a little action, but you can always say no and keep hidden. Just keep that in mind."

She steps into her room and closes the door behind her with a swing of her hips.

"I'm in charge." I find myself repeating these words all the way back over to my computer.

Taking a seat, I pull up the information for the website and just stare at the screen.

Putting on my big girl panties, I grab the sticky note from the side of the monitor and type in my login info, almost afraid of what might pop up.

My eyes go wide as all of the info uploads along with ten different men's profiles, each one attached with a picture. Every single one except for his . . . Lynx Kade.

"Seriously," I mumble to myself. "This guy is so damn good that he doesn't even need a pic to get noticed?" I let out a sarcastic laugh and sip my wine, while checking out the other guys of the Alpha rooms.

A few of them are just okay looking, six of them are insanely hot and one has no face, yet has the most five star reviews.

Yes . . . every guy has a star rating on their performance, along with testimonies from their clients.

This website does not mess around.

Curious about just how much these gorgeous men would cost me, I click on the prices and my mouth drops.

"Holy. Fuck."

Fifteen-minute session: $500.00.

Thirty-minute session: $800.00.

Hour long session: $1,500.00.

No wonder Remi is always low on money. What the actual fuck. I should kick her ass for this and my own ass for even considering it.

Picking my jaw back up, I stare at the pictures, trying to decide who's profile to click on first.

Blaze's light hair, short beard and muscular frame pop out at me, so I click on his profile and read the first five-star review.

After three months of not being able to reach climax, one fifteen-minute session with Blaze had my pussy aching so badly for release that it only took me fifteen seconds of touching myself to have one of the best orgasms of my life. I haven't been this turned on since I was in my early twenties and I'm now well into my forties. Well worth the $500.00 and I've decided to make this a monthly thing after this.

~Anonymous

"Well . . . okay then."

I swallow hard and close down his profile, telling myself that if a woman in her forties can do this and not feel dirty, that maybe it isn't so bad after all.

I skim through a few more of the men's profiles and reviews, before finally caving in and clicking on this mysterious Mr. Lynx Kade's.

The first thing I notice is that his prices are different. Higher.

Fifteen-minute session: $700.00.

Thirty-minute session: $1,100.00.

Hour long session: $2,000.00.

"Okay, now I'm positive Remi is trying to make my ass find a second job by introducing me to this site."

Blowing out a breath, I click on the top five-star review, knowing that there's no way I'll be able to close out of this website without seeing what the girls are saying about this *top Alpha*.

I have never experienced something so HOT and EROTIC in my life. Before I decided to give the Alpha boys a shot, I heard that Lynx had the most beautiful dick I'd ever lay eyes on and oh how true that statement is. Not to mention that he has the body of a god. I'd give my left tit just to be able to touch him and do the dirty things that I asked him to do to himself. I paid for a thirty-minute session and it only took me five to get off and realize that I'm addicted to watching this man. Looks like I'll add my name back to the waiting list. I don't care if it takes two months to watch him again. He's worth it. Trust me ladies. I'd spend a whole paycheck if I had to.

~Kikiknight87

Wow! Can a man's dick really be as beautiful as these women claim? I can't help but to wonder.

Telling myself that I need to finish this stupid web design by tonight, I close out of the Alpha website and pretend that my mind hasn't been on it for the last hour, while trying to focus.

My whole body is aching to see this beautiful dicked man and curious if his face will be just as beautiful as his dick is claimed to be.

I have to be stupid to even be considering this right now . . .

Chapter TWO

Lynx

"I TOLD YOU ASSHOLES TO be here by nine," I growl into the phone. "Is that so hard? We have to get the house done today because every single one of you have full schedules tonight."

"Alright, alright. I'll be there in a fuckin' few, Man. I had a rough night." Blaze is one of my top guys and I need his room ready before I can even think about the rest of them.

"I know what kind of night you had. Get your ass here quick or I'm giving you a fucking metal folding chair and a computer to work with. You can set your naked balls right against the cold metal as far as I'm concerned."

"Damn. Is this the shit I have to look forward to?"

I need to chill the fuck out. I've been stressed trying to get the club and the website ready for the grand opening. It isn't enough that I just bought *Club Royal*. Hell no. I have a death wish and decided to move my guys here and try to expand my own business.

"You know I'm just stressed to get it all going. Just get here and help me unload these trucks and then you can be gone every damn morning if you want."

"I hear you. Seriously just walked to my truck in my underwear just for you, Man. See you in about five minutes."

I was lucky enough to find the perfect land near the club to build a house big enough to move us all in to. I didn't have any luck finding one in the area that would work for us. I wasn't looking for much, just one big enough for six men to live in and also including enough spare rooms for my guys that only need to be here a few days out of the week.

It's what happens when you start a business that literally explodes with new clients every day. I can't keep up with all the calls even though we've raised the prices. I could just keep adding more guys to the group, but honestly I can't fucking stand babysitting anyone. These guys are genuine and on a normal day, I know business will run smoothly with all of them on board.

They like that paycheck too much to fuck me over. Not many people can say they work for a few hours and bring in a minimum of five grand every night. Hell, that's after they take the company commission off the top.

It was just supposed to be a little side money to help me get my bike fixed. I had no idea it would turn into a million-dollar business in just a few months.

I may regret letting them all live in the house, but for now that's part of our agreement. I can see this being one constant party after another and there's nothing wrong with that. It'll just bring more exposure to the business.

Club Royal should be a giant tax write off for me, which I'm going to need a few of. I did bring in new management to help me run it, so hopefully I can remain a silent owner there and keep my focus where the real money is.

Alphachat.com- where you can Pay for Play time with any one of us guys. I'm still taking my own calls as of now, but that may eventually change. I haven't decided what else I'd do with my time, so making money sounds like the best plan for now.

I meet the movers at the end of the drive and give them a tour of the house. Their comments about the size of all the rooms only reminds me of the meeting with the building contractor. He was shocked to see how many large master bedrooms I wanted built into the plan. I'm glad I stuck to my vision, because they all get a great sized room to be creative with their clients. All the houses on the market had tiny extra bedrooms and none of them had as many as we need.

After I show the movers where each of the rooms are, I get out of their way and gladly take a few calls out by the pool.

My phone rings again with the same damn number I've been sending to voice mail all morning.

"Sadie. I told you I'm fucking done. You're a money hungry whore and the second you heard I was moving, you hooked up with my damn brother."

"But Lynx. I was drunk. He acts so much like you and it just felt right." Her dramatic tears cause me to pull my phone away from my ear and consider throwing it in the pool. I let her continue for a while longer before I put it back up to my ear. "and . . . I just felt like I was close to you when I was with him. Let me come see you in your new place."

"Stop fucking talking. You will never get past my gates. I don't give a fuck how much you cry. Enjoy my brother. Maybe he can buy you a nice dress with some of that money he makes stealing shit." I hit end and toss my phone onto one of the lounge chairs, unable to deal with her shit right now.

My brother is a real piece of work. I tried to give him a chance at earning his own money, but he has 'boundaries'. I get that he has limits, but to say that, when he fucking strong arms people to bring home his paycheck, makes me sick.

Sadie deserves him. She's money hungry as hell. I knew the

reason she was sniffing around my dick the second I met her. I've never been one to let that stop me from a few fucks, but I'm not moving her here like she wants. Especially not after she fucked my brother to get at me.

I don't do liars. If someone lies to me, they may as well consider themselves written off. "You made your bed bitch, now lay in it," I grumble to myself, furious that she even had the fucking nerve to call again.

I hear the back door fly open just as I get near the waterfall flowing into the pool. I had the hot tub set behind it on purpose, imagining that I may want some damn privacy once in a while.

"I finally made it! What can I do for you, Big Guy?" Nash is my newest entertainer. He's the smooth cowboy that all the ladies are just catching on to. I hear his Southern drawl and I can practically hear the dollar signs flashing through my head.

"Just get your room prepped for live shows tonight. Your schedule is cram packed since you've been traveling the last few days."

"That's easy. Did you see my props delivery yet?"

"Not yet. Hopefully it'll be here in the next few hours."

I can only imagine the props he'll bring into the house. I'm actually pissed that I didn't think of the whole country look for myself. I could've changed up my look a little for my repeat callers.

"Alright. Just holler if you need me to help with anything." Just then the door opens with Blaze and Knox strutting toward us. Blaze is still in his underwear.

"Am I going to have to watch you prance around in those fucking panties all the damn time?"

"Shit. This is your fault. You're the one that had me talking out loud. She threw my ass out the window because of you."

"Where the hell where you?" I have to ask, even though I'm

afraid to know.

"Some college girl's house. She lives with her parents." He runs his hand over his grinning mouth.

"Can't you find someone normal? Tell me she's at least in her damn twenties."

"Yeah she is."

I'm going to have to add that shit to the house rules today.

"Alright. Get your rooms done and make a test call to make sure everything is working before the tech guys leave. They should be here any minute to help. Then we'll have a house meeting at seven. Calls start at eight tonight and most of us are running 'til three."

"Are you always all business? Cuz, I'm gonna have fun convincing you to cut loose." Blaze starts to harass me and I let it slide this time. I know I'm the focused type, but I have to be to run a business like this.

"That's why we're going to plan one helluva party next weekend. We'll talk about it tonight, so get your shit done so I can relax."

I watch the three of them laugh and joke all the way back into the house. A smile finally crosses my face knowing that we're almost there. Now we'll just get to enjoy the ride.

It's quite a trip back to my bedroom. I did that on purpose just to have some privacy if I ever do want to have someone over. Not to mention that I don't want to constantly hear these guys banging walls or sending moans through the night. It's bad enough that I don't usually get done with my calls 'til after two.

I close the door and hit the remote to turn on my big screen that's mounted just above my computer monitor. I didn't opt for the large computer screen because there's no reason to. When I'm working, I'm focused on the big titties bouncing on the big one. I'm not afraid to admit it. It takes porn to help me get hard when I'm entertaining.

Very few of the women allow me to view them during a session and most of the ones that do. . . . I wish they wouldn't. It does nothing for my dick.

There are some things that just can't be unseen. Shaking my head trying to lose the memories, I find the best porn channel to freeze it on. I click 'top rated videos', then select the first one to pop up. It's a threesome, that works for me. Now to test the complicated shit.

I know I need to check my own tech work for sure, so I log in to the website. I'm hoping my loyal stable Vivian will be on and can accept a quick call. Dialing her number, I move into view once she answers.

"Hey, Handsome. Tell me you missed ole' Viv and you need some lovin'."

"Just testing all the equipment in the new place. Thought I'd give you a special treat since you're one of my loyal girls." She turns on her own camera and I get to see her in her play room. Her tits are bursting over the corset lingerie she's wearing and my mind instantly flashes to the first night I fucked her.

"Well show me your equipment and I'll let you know if it still works for me." Her sexy smile pulls a smirk from me while she moves across her bed into position.

Her crotch-less panties leave nothing to the imagination and it's a matter of seconds before I'm watching her finger herself. "Are you just gonna watch me tonight? I'll have to start charging you for a show if that's the case."

I stand in front of the camera and slowly unbutton my jeans. She likes me to move slow.

I rub the bulge showing through my jeans just to remind her how far it reaches.

"I remember feeling that cock of yours, Lynx." She puts her

lips around a dildo and slowly sucks on it a few times before she begins rubbing the tip of it over her clit.

By then I have my cock in my hand and I'm reaching for the coconut oil. It's my favorite lube for show, not to mention it gives me a soft dick that the ladies appreciate in their mouth.

"You wish it was your dick, don't ya, baby?" She slowly slides the blue vibrating cock between her legs and throws her head back just slightly as she adjusts to the size. She has one of the exact molds of my cock. It was a onetime deal to get more business and she went crazy trying to win one even though she's had the real thing a few times.

"It is my dick." I slide my fingers around my cock and begin stroking slowly as I watch her get off without another word. She's moaning and gyrating her hips like she's actually riding me. *Fuck*. At this rate it's going to be a long night.

This is what happens when I haven't fucked for a few days.

Fuck me . . .

Chapter THREE

Rebel

I CAN'T BELIEVE I'M DOING THIS. I may need my head examined. "Do you think I should even go in?" I've been parked across the street for at least thirty minutes talking to Remi about *Club Royal*. The parking lot is full of cars, so I know someone will be around to take my application, but I just can't seem to make myself go in.

"Yes. What the hell, Rebel. How did you even get named that anyway?" I swear she finds it entertaining to put me in situations that are uncomfortable to me. I know I'm not much of a rebel, but there are times I can be. She's just never really experienced that side of me.

I guess I kind of grew out of all the club crap a few years ago. It didn't take me long to realize the bar scene is not my best place to shine.

I close the mirror flap on the visor and adjust my dress as I try to decide if this is all worth it. Yes, I need a different job, but do I really want to head this direction with my career?

"Alright, I'm going in. Have your phone just in case I want to strangle you when I leave here." Her laughter echoes through my speakers as I drive to a closer parking spot.

"I will. Just call me when you leave."

"Have fun on your date."

"You know I will. Bye, Babe." I'm jealous of her free spirited ass getting a date practically every night, but some of the crap she has to deal with is insane. I wouldn't trade her places for the world with some of the creeps she deals with. It's hard to find a normal guy these days and right now that's not something I have time to deal with.

I slam the door to my Jeep and adjust my dress one last time. My hand brushes my leg beneath my skirt and I instantly wish I would've worn the dress I had picked out myself. This one is Remi's and I'm positive it's shorter on me than it is on her. Of course my big boobs might have something to do with that. No matter how 'minimizing' the bra says it is, it never hides these girls enough.

The doors are intricate and I can't help but admire the details of the front entrance again. A man in a suit greets me at the next set of doors and the sound of music blares from behind him.

"Good evening. Welcome to *Club Royal*. Can I get your name?" His deep voice surprises me and I try not to look at his big bulging arms showing through his jacket.

"Rebel Brooks. I'm here to turn in an application." He looks at the papers in my hand and steps out from behind his podium. Opening the door, he allows me through and instantly all of my senses are overwhelmed with the beauty of this place. When I came here a few days ago, I didn't get past the entrance, before someone spotted me and handed me the paper work.

I stop mid step and frantically look for the obvious place to drop my information off, but don't see one. The smell of cologne and alcohol linger in the air as I glance over the dance floor that's full of gorgeous people dancing.

I side step a couple walking toward me and decide to sit on the only bar stool available on the end. The first guy to notice me is a bartender, filling someone's whiskey glass well past the normal level. He smiles and nods his head in my direction. My nerves begin to explode and I contemplate leaving the bar before he begins walking toward the end I'm sitting at. "What can I get ya?"

"Oh I'm sorry. I'm not drinking. Just need to talk to a manager."

"He's not around; what can I help you with?" His eyes move over me and I instantly try to hide my cleavage behind my arm in some nonchalant way that I'm sure appears ridiculous to anyone looking.

He's gorgeous. I can't stand the chills that slide across my chest as his eyes do.

"I . . . I just need to turn in this application." He grabs a towel and reaches for the papers still clenched in my hand. I hesitate just slightly wondering if this is the actual manager himself. He's not at all some fat baldy like I'd imagined.

"You got any bartender experience?" He leans against the bar facing me as he thumbs through each of my papers.

"I do." I sit straight up on my stool as a line of people pass through behind me. This place is packed and I can't even imagine trying to keep all the drinks straight in a place like this. It seems as though they'd all be after a perfect tasting drink.

"I see you have experience with management." He sets the application down in front of me.

"I have a little."

"Alright. Give me a few minutes and I'll take you back to him." I glance at his name tag and catch the name 'Knox'. *That's a unique name.*

I try not to stare at the men behind the bar, but I'm finding it difficult. There are three of them and they all seem to be gorgeous. It's weird for me to think like this about one guy, let alone three standing together.

This is probably a terrible idea. There's no way in hell I could work with men that look like this on a nightly basis and stay sane.

"Come with me. He said he'd meet with you." I make the mental note that he totally lied to me when he said the manager wasn't here, but of course I'm not going to bring that up. I'm just hoping to land a position as a cocktail waitress, even if it's only for a few months.

He opens the hidden door to an entire back area of the club. The long hallway is quiet and even the music is silenced back here. I'm working hard not to watch this guy's ass while he leads the way, but it's hard not to. *Damn why does he have to get me flustered before I meet the fat guy?*

He stops us in front of a door that's slightly open, just in time for me to catch a man yelling into his phone.

"What the fuck do you not understand about silent owner? That means I don't want to have to deal with the shit in the club on the daily. I hired you to be here and you're not. I had two fucking bartenders not show tonight and a house full of paying customers. This is the shit you're supposed to deal with. You're fucking fired. I'll mail your damn paycheck to you." He slams the phone on the desk twice before he sets it on the receiver. He turns before he sees us and dials someone on his cell phone.

"We're fucking stuck here. Clear my schedule tonight. I'll send Blaze back now and if any of the guys have time, send them to help get this shit dealt with." The tension in the room is practically suffocating me. This is a terrible time to try to talk to him.

"Hey, Boss. I have someone here who wants to turn in an

application. Thought you'd maybe want to see her." He turns his head quickly, allowing his eyes to travel down my entire body and back up before he does anything. He takes a deep breath and slides his hand over his cheek and through his hair in an obvious moment of frustration, then speaks to the bartender named Knox. "Thanks. Get Blaze and both of you get out of here. Tell Nash I'll be there in a minute and Levi is on his way."

"Sure thing." He guides me to a chair sitting in front of the desk and whispers "Good luck" under his breath before he winks at me.

I sit slowly as I watch the angry, but insanely sexy, boss pace along the side wall of the room before he returns to his desk.

His dark hair, amber eyes and muscular build, have me practically drowning in a puddle of drool. A black button-down has never looked better than it does on this man. It's fitted perfectly to his broad chest with the sleeves rolled up just enough to display tattoos on both of his forearms.

"I'm sorry you had to hear me yelling, but I just fired the manager because he's a stupid fuck and can't seem to do his job. What qualifications do you have?" His abrupt tone startles me and instantly I'm nervous and can't stand how jittery I sound when I begin to talk.

"I'm actually a graphic designer, but looking for a part-time job to help me until I get on my feet with my own business a little."

"So what you're saying . . . You have zero skills in bartending and you're not here to save my night."

"I actually do have experience bartending." I didn't really want to go that direction for this job, but it seems like that's what he's in desperate need of tonight.

"Perfect. Can you start right now?" I look down at my dress and then back up at him. I catch his eyes focused on my chest, but this time I force myself not to awkwardly try to hide it.

I wanted a job tonight, just had no idea I'd literally be starting this very second.

"Sure. Why not." He quickly moves from behind the desk and starts for the door.

"Good because we're shorthanded and it'll just be you and I behind the VIP bar tonight." His ass is even better than the other guy's was and it's causing me to bite my bottom lip and force my eyes to the floor. I can't believe what I've got myself into. Can I really work next to this man when I haven't done this in years?

I've lost my damn mind.

Chapter FOUR

Lynx

I STAND BACK FOR A second, now that the crowd in the VIP section has died down a bit, and secretly admire the fact that she does indeed have skills behind the bar. She's also proven herself as a professional working within this elite section of the club. I've heard a few of these rich assholes can be giant dicks to bartenders back here.

I'm glad I gave her a chance tonight. I never trust anyone on their word alone, unless I have a very good reason to. So knowing that there was no fucking way I'd be leaving here tonight before the VIP parties were done, I asked Rebel to start tonight, on the spot.

My eyes have been glued to her beautiful fucking body every chance that I get, when not having to deal with my own drinks. Partly because I had to evaluate her performance and the other part . . . well . . . fuck me. It was for my own pleasure.

If all my callers had a face as innocently beautiful as hers with a body that screamed sin and sex; I wouldn't need porn in the background to get off.

I'd love to spend hours running my tongue over every curve

of her body, tasting every single one of her fuckin' sins until my tongue goes numb. I wouldn't let up until I've traced all the sexy tattoos down her left arm and finished my search for any that are hidden. I can see the single daisy on her shoulder and it's just asking to be looked at closer.

Plus, after three hours of watching her take orders and pour them like a damn pro, there's no way I'm letting her go without giving her the job she came here seeking.

Club Royal needs someone skilled and reliable so I won't have to spend my nights filling in and getting seen by old or possible callers.

Hell . . . it's hard enough even showing my face in here without being stopped every damn second. Put my ass behind the bar and it takes twenty minutes to complete one transaction and get the women to let me take other orders.

That's exactly why I didn't want myself and the guys behind the bars tonight, but some dumb-fuck decided he had better shit to do than be here doing the job I pay his ass for.

There are no second chances with me. Fuck me over and you're fucked. Simple as that.

Not only did he fuck me over by not showing tonight, but he under scheduled staff, leaving me no choice but to call my guys in and hold the place down, when two of the bartenders that *he* hired, called in.

Watching Rebel fan herself off, my eyes land on the sweat running down her neck and falling between her sexy as fuck tits.

I won't deny that I wish it were me making her sweat right now. At least then it'd be worth every last fucking drop.

"You need a break?" I ask, causing her to look over at me and realize that I'm watching her practically melt. "I'll have one of the guys turn the air up."

Smiling shyly, she shakes her head and continues to fan

herself, focusing on her glistening chest now.

Fuck me . . .

"I'm fine. It's just been a while since I've moved around this much." She smiles small and arches her back, not realizing what it's doing to my dick as she slowly wipes a cold, wet paper towel down her neck, squeezing out water to cool her off. "I just need a few minutes to breathe and maybe a glass of water."

My tongue mindlessly runs across my lower lip, before I bite it and growl under my breath, as the water drips down her body, disappearing below the top of her white dress.

"Take a few minutes and take care of yourself. We're about done here for the night. The boys can handle the crowd at the main bar after midnight."

"Thank you." Giving me an appreciative smile, she walks away, pouring herself a glass of ice water and downing it so fast that she chokes on it and begins coughing.

The cute little way she blushes from embarrassment and looks down at the ground, has me wanting to fuck the embarrassment right out of her and give her some confidence that a woman as damn beautiful as her should have.

"Need some help?" Watching her chest rise and fall with each hard breath, I step close enough to let her know that I am willing to give her anything she wants me to.

She shakes her head and waves me off. "Believe it or not, I'm used to this." She laughs softly. "My roommate could vouch for me."

Smiling, I keep my eyes on her tilting her glass back again, while picking up the bar phone and calling over to the main bar. Nash answers it. "We're closing down over here. Tell Levi to keep it in his fucking pants after I leave. I'll review those cameras every damn night after close if I have to just to make sure you dipshits keep my club sanitary and come free. Leave that shit for your own personal play rooms."

"Brought the trusted cowboy hat tonight, Big Guy," he says in his slow Southern drawl. "Levi doesn't have a shot. Same goes for Rome."

"It won't stop his ass from trying. I want you in charge. Call me if you need me to come back. Just make sure it's a damn good reason . . ."

"Gotcha. Gotta go, Boss."

Hanging up the receiver, I run my hand over the stubble from not shaving for a few days, and let out a relieved breath that things went a lot smoother tonight than I had originally thought.

When my eyes search out my newest bartender, she's bent over cleaning, her dress riding up just enough to show the bottom of her curvy ass cheeks.

Leaning against the register, I take a moment to admire the curve of her ass and imagine the dirty things I'd do if I dropped to my knees right now and spread her legs. I bet she's never had anyone that close to her ass before.

She looks too clean. A man like me would dirty her up after just one night.

"You did good tonight. I'll have the boys finish up so you can get out of here."

"Really?" She releases the towel and smiles with confidence. It's sexy as hell on her. "I was extremely nervous I'd screw up and disappoint you. I really need this job right now."

"You definitely didn't disappoint. You'd know it if you did."

Her eyes take a moment to look me up and down, now that she's had a few moments to breathe and calm down.

As soon as she takes notice of the smirk on my face, she clears her throat and pulls her eyes away, looking embarrassed at being caught. "When would you like me to come back in? I can pretty much work my other job around being here at *Club*

Royal."

"Good." I place my hand on the small of her back and guide her away from the bar and out of the VIP section. "I'm going to want you here a lot, starting tomorrow at two so you can take a tour and get a chance to get familiar with the club, while it's not as busy. Pay is twenty dollars an hour, plus tips." Reaching in my pocket, I pull out the tip money from the VIP bar, that I collected after we slowed down, and hand it all to her. "First check will be next Friday."

Looking surprised, she looks down at the wad of cash in her hand. "Whoa, that's a lot of money. Did you take your share? Here." She holds out the money as if to hand it back.

I shake my head. "I don't accept tip money."

Walking behind the main bar, I open the drawer and pull out the drink list, holding it out for her. "What's this?" she asks, while reaching for it.

"A list of our popular drinks. The night will go smoother if you can memorize most of them."

"Gotcha." Her eyes widen as she starts looking it over. "That's a lot to remember, but I'm a pretty quick learner."

"I'll be happy to help, Baby Girl?" Levi appears next to her with a cocky look on his baby face. "I'll help you with anything you want."

"The fuck you will," I growl out. "Take care of your own shit first. You have two women waiting on drinks. Get on it. Now."

Looking Rebel over with a quickness, he lifts a brow, showing interest, before turning away and getting his ass back to work.

"Ignore these assholes. Some of them need a good kick in the balls sometimes. You won't be seeing much of them, anyway."

Smiling with amusement, she holds up the drink menu.

"Thank you so much again for giving me a chance. I promise you won't regret it."

With that, she walks away and I quickly grab my shit, getting out of here as fast as I can.

I still have a long night ahead of me . . .

PREPARING FOR THE ONLY CALL I'll be taking tonight, I turn on the big screen TV and make sure it's on silent, before I log in to my website.

Within five minutes, a chat comes in from username *SassyandPlayful69*.

She's a repeat customer of mine and not one to get excited over; one of the many women that never show their faces, but the good thing is that she keeps it simple and only purchases fifteen-minutes sessions.

It's little work, well worth the *$700.00*.

With as tired as I am right now, I'm good with short and simple. I'll take that shit and ride with it, thankful that I won't have to do any crazy shit on camera tonight.

Accepting the call, I sit back on my leather couch and begin running my hands over my body, before she even gives me my first demand.

I don't need it anymore. I'm pretty good at memorizing what each and every regular gets off on.

"Looking good tonight, Lynx." Her voice comes through on the black screen, sounding hot and heavy already. "Oh yeah, you know how I like it."

"I know you like it like this . . ." Undoing my pants, I yank them down just enough for her to see the shape of my hard cock, through the fabric of my boxer briefs. "Nice and fucking hard. So fucking hard in these tight as fuck briefs."

"Mmmm . . . so tight," she moans, as I stand and drop my jeans, completely. "Rub it for me, Lynx."

Closing my eyes, my mind somehow drifts to Rebel and how damn hot she looked in that sexy little dress tonight. My dick instantly gets rock hard, flexing in my hand as I rub it nice and slow.

"You weren't lying," she says with excitement. "It's so hard. Let me see it. Take your briefs off."

I lower them and pull my cock out. I rub my hand over it a few times, stroking it before turning to the side and giving her a view of its length.

"It's so damn big." Her breathing picks up and I know without even seeing her that she's touching herself. "Stroke it. Stroke it hard and fast."

Letting my mind drift back to Rebel, I squirt a little of my favorite oil in my palm and rub it over my cock, before quickly stroking it to thoughts of me bending her all over the bar and sliding my cock between her perfect ass.

I'd love to make her scream.

Within a couple of minutes, I hear extremely loud breathing coming from *SassyandPlayful69*, before she moans so damn hard and good that I get off, shooting my come everywhere, while picturing it were Rebel moaning for me.

I'm lost in my own little world for a few seconds, before I hear her breathy voice again, bringing my ass back to reality. "You never disappoint, do you?"

"No and I won't."

"You don't have to tell me, Big Boy. I'll be back in two weeks for some more of your fine ass."

"I know you will," I say with a hint of a smile, before the chat session ends and cuts her off, right as she's about to say something back.

Fuck . . . Looks like Rebel saved my ass in more ways than one tonight . . .

Chapter FIVE

Rebel

I'VE SPENT THE LAST FOUR hours at the computer, drowning myself in caffeine, while trying to get caught up, since I wasn't expecting to start work at the club last night.

When the boss asked me to start on the spot, I about died. I was nervous, sweaty and already tired, but when a man with that much power asks you to do something . . . you say yes, and I did. I didn't even hesitate for one second, knowing that it's not easy getting into an exclusive club such as *Club Royal*.

I've worked at bars in the past, but not since I was twenty-two. I turned twenty-five three months ago so I was scared out of my mind that I'd mess up every drink and cause him to fire me in front of the whole club.

In just the short amount of time that I bartended at *Club Royal* last night, I served more customers than I did in any seven or eight-hour shift that I worked at any other bar, but surprisingly it all came back to me naturally, saving my butt from embarrassment.

At the end of the night when he handed me that tip money, I had to force my mouth from dropping open. Never in my wildest dreams would I have imagined making that much money in under four hours.

"Did you seriously make almost five-hundred last night?" Remi has been sitting on the couch, repeatedly counting my tip money from the bar. "That's crazy. What the hell kind of drinks are they serving at that place? And do I even want to know the average price of one is?"

Laughing at her bugged out eyes, I close down the computer and take another sip of my coffee. "Whatever is there is from what I made last night. Not a cent of that came from my purse . . ." Standing up, I walk to the kitchen to wash out my mug. I have less than an hour now, before I have to be at the club for the tour. "The menu is on the table, Remi. They were just regular drinks at the normal price. I haven't been shown how to make the premium ones yet, but that's a list of the most popular ones, I'm guessing. These people drink like fish. I seriously lost count of how many I poured tonight."

"I think I'm still sleeping." She shakes her head really fast as if trying to wake up. "You hit the jackpot with this job, Babe. Just imagine the kind of money you can bring in for a full shift. You'll only need to do graphic designing when you want, instead of taking on every client you can get. I know it weighs on you. You might enjoy it, but not enough to depend on it to pay bills."

"I do enjoy it," I respond. "But yeah, depending on it to pay the bills does kind of make me despise it sometimes. Working at the club will hopefully bring me in enough money to get a savings account started so I won't have to depend on it, but do it because I enjoy it. You know . . ."

She yawns, while looking over the top of the couch at me. "Exactly. You struggled so much in the first months, that you spent way too much time on that damn computer. You need to get out of the house. This job will do you good."

"That's what I'm hoping."

Remi reaches for the remote and turns on the TV, getting comfortable since it's her day off. "So, was the boss as awful as you imagined? That's got to be the only down to this job, huh? Is he some huge asshole that rode your ass all night, breathing down your neck?"

I swallow hard and my heart speeds up at just the mention of that insanely beautiful man.

My whole body overheated every single time his eyes landed on me and had me almost melting every time he spoke.

His voice was so sexy: husky and demanding power with every word that left his full set of lips. How I managed to function around him is beyond me. I couldn't even manage to ask the man his name, even though I wanted so badly to know. I didn't want anything making the night or myself any more awkward, so I waited for him to give it, but he never did.

"I'm going to guess by the way you're biting your bottom lip that he wasn't the short, stubby man with a potbelly that you imagined."

I shake my head, while walking past her, realizing that I need to be fast if I want to take a shower before I have to leave. "Not exactly. I'll tell you about him later. I'm short on time."

"Where are you going?" she yells after me. "Do you work today?"

"No," I yell back, while gathering my clothes for a shower. "I think I'm just taking a tour of the building since I didn't get to last night."

"Alright . . . I'll tell you about my crappy date later."

I stop in the doorway of the bathroom. "Shit. I'm sorry, Remi. You started asking me about the club and . . ."

"Oh it's nothing exciting. Trust me. I'd rather hear about the club, than relive the events of last night this early. I'll be here on the couch *all* day, ready to talk when you get back."

"I'll be ready to listen. I promise."

"Doesn't matter if you're not. You'll be hearing it anyway. Now take a shower. You stink like sweat, liquor and . . ." she sniffs the air. "Some pretty sexy cologne."

Holding my arm to my nose, I take a whiff and exhale with a small moan, remembering the excitement that coursed through my body the few times that we bumped into each other, our bodies brushing.

I fought hard, trying my best to not let him see how attracted I was to him, but if I'm honest with myself, I swear he was checking me out just as much as I was secretly admiring his rock hard body.

"Getting in the shower now."

A MIXTURE OF EXCITEMENT AND nervousness courses through me as I pull up in the parking lot of *Club Royal* and turn my Jeep off.

I have no idea who's going to be giving me this tour, but I'm kind of hoping it's not *him*. I'm not sure how much more of him I can see without seeming like a creeper, the way my eyes can't help but to follow every muscle of that man's glorious body.

As much as I tried to hide it last night, he caught me at the end of the night just as my eyes were lowering to the noticeable sized bulge in his pants.

He wasn't even hard, I could tell that, yet he looked so *big*. I noticed that quite a few times throughout the night, which is partly why I was sweaty and desperate for water. It really wasn't the constant drink pouring.

It was him.

After getting past the man working the front door, I spend the next thirty minutes, following some beautiful pink haired girl around that goes by the name Envy.

Not sure if that's her real name, but I can see why she goes by it. She's so gorgeous, that even I can't help but to stare.

"So you're pretty familiar with the VIP bar and the main one now? I was told you spent a few hours last night at the VIP area. Do you need more time to check out the main bar or are you ready for the break room, where we keep our stuff and get ready before our shifts?"

I nod my head, while taking one last look at the main bar, realizing that it's set up a lot like the VIP one, but just bigger. "I'm ready."

She smiles and begins walking. "You learn pretty quickly, Sweets. Come on."

Following her through the bar and then a large wooden door, she takes me down the same hall that the boss' office was at.

My eyes land on the closed door and my heart speeds up.

"That's the owner's office. I've never seen him because he likes to keep private so I'm not sure if you'll get the pleasure of meeting him. I swear he has some secret way of getting in this place, because I never see him enter, but sometimes the light is on in his room. I don't know why, but I'm dying to get a glimpse."

And you'll die once you get one too . . . I about did.

I continue following her down the hall, until she stops in front of a door and pushes it open. "I usually like to show up about twenty minutes before my shift begins so that it gives me time to make my way back here, lock my things away and prepare for the night. You might want to think about doing the same. The management here doesn't take being late lightly."

She points to the lockers. "You can put your personal

belongings in one of those and grab the key number from the drawer. You're going to want to keep it on you so no one else can get in your things. *Not* that you need to worry. There are security cameras all over this damn place. It's just to make us feel comfortable with leaving our purses and whatever else is important to us back here while we work."

"Makes sense," I reply. "Wish some of the other bars I've worked at would've had something like this."

She raises a brow. "Did they make you shove it next to the register? Been there and it sucks. You never know who you can trust. Especially at a damn bar."

"Yes. And very true."

There's a small awkward silence since I have no idea what all I'm supposed to be doing here right now. I just watch her, waiting for her to point me in the next direction, but she just stands there, looking me over.

"Will you be teaching me some of the premium drinks?"

She smiles down at my worn out Converse shoes and then up at me. "Nope, especially not dressed like that, sweetie. You'll be hearing from someone else when they want you to come in and learn the drinks. I'm guessing either before the bar opens one day this week or after it closes. At least that's how Ben did it. His ass is no longer here so I have no clue who's taking over management and what's going to float their boat."

"Alright . . . so we're done?"

"Yup. You'll get paid for the hour you were here and expect a phone call soon." She points toward the door. "I've gotta get back and help Brit. Good luck, Babe." She winks and walks out the door.

I take a few seconds to look around my new break room, admiring how comfy it looks with its black, leather couch and recliner chairs. It even has a Keurig.

Thank goodness for that . . .

After I get back home, I somehow end up falling asleep for over four hours, before Remi wakes me up, telling me all the details of her horrible date last night.

Apparently, he spent a majority of the date talking about his ex-girlfriend that cheated on him and now wants him to take her back. He got shitfaced and begged Remi to come in when she drove him home in *his* car and then took a taxi back to hers. Fear of nights like that is exactly why I don't date much.

After Remi retires to her room, I jump back on the computer to finish some work.

It's now just past eleven and I'm so damn exhausted and sexually frustrated, that I want to scream.

I don't know what's going on with me, but ever since working the VIP section the other night with my new boss, I haven't been able to stop thinking about sex.

I keep picturing his strong hands on my body as his beautiful lips run along my skin, tasting me. What I wouldn't give to see if his dick is really as big as it appeared through those thin dress pants.

My thoughts make me feel dirty.

"He's your boss, Rebel," I remind myself, while clicking through my emails, deleting all of the spam.

I freeze and my heart starts racing with excitement when I come across an email from *Alphachat.com*.

The email came in at three o'clock today, letting me know that Lynx Kade has an opening tonight at midnight and I have until eleven thirty to confirm or deny.

"Shit, what do I do?" I look up at the clock to see that I have less than five minutes to make my decision.

My whole body is screaming to click the accept button, but my head is telling me that this whole thing is crazy . . . and dirty.

Extremely dirty . . . but exciting. I need excitement.

Swallowing, I make a rash decision, knowing that time is running out and I have no clue if I'll get another opportunity if I decline.

Remi made it very clear that this Lynx guy has a waiting list and can sometimes take weeks or even months to get a private session.

He has to be good. At least for my aching body's sake; let's hope.

Hitting accept, I fight to catch my breath the whole time, while typing in my credit card info. I can't believe that I'm actually paying $700 for fifteen minutes of play with some guy.

"I'm insane. I have to be."

Quickly shutting down the desktop computer, I rush to my room for privacy and take a seat at my desk, opening up my laptop and starting it.

Reaching for my bottle of water, I undo the lid and take a huge gulp, while logging back into the site and watching as the minutes countdown to midnight.

The closer it gets to midnight, the dirtier, but more excited I feel.

I can't deny that it gives me a rush, knowing that I'm about to watch some stranger touch himself for me.

"Oh fuck . . . Oh fuck." I suck in a deep breath once it counts down to the last minute. "I'm really doing this."

In a panic, I double check to make sure that I have both the volume and the screen turned off so I can stay completely anonymous.

I calm down a little and take a deep breath in just enough time for a picture to come up on the screen of a black, leather couch.

After a few seconds, a hard, muscled body appears in front

of the screen, before my boss' face comes into view.

"Oh my fucking God!" My hands go up to cover my mouth as I watch him adjust his computer, before taking a seat on the couch. I can't believe my boss does this on the side and that I'm about to see everything he has to offer.

He's wearing a black V-neck shirt that is clinging to every muscle and a pair of sweats, showing off his muscular thighs. His hair is messy and he looks so damn good that I want to taste him.

"I see you're a first timer," his husky voice comes through, making my thighs clench. "Tell me what you want me to do."

"I'm not doing this. I'm not doing this." I begin typing, unable to stop myself. "I am doing this . . . I can't believe I'm doing this."

Badgirl@heart ~ Take your shirt off, please.

A sexy smirk appears on his face. "No need to be nice."

Standing up, he grips the back of his shirt and slowly pulls it over his head, exposing the sexiest, firmest chest I've ever laid eyes on.

"Oh. My. God."

Tossing his shirt aside, he lifts a brow and lowers the waist of his sweats, just enough to expose the very defined muscles, leading down to the bulge that I've been *dying* to see. My eyes are glued to the tattoos across his lower stomach as I lean closer to read, "Veni. Vidi. Vici." I know exactly what that means. I came. I saw. I conquered. *Holy fuck that's hot.*

"What now, *BadGirl@heart?* You going to show me just how fucking bad you can be?"

My heart's beating so damn hard as I type this next part, that I have to erase it a few times and rewrite it because I keep messing up.

BadGirl@heart ~ Slowly run your hands down your abs and

then lower your sweats.

"So bad girl likes it slow . . . and hopefully hard."

Starting with his defined chest, he slowly and teasingly runs his hands down his body, going lower until he reaches his abs. He then grips the top of his sweats, teasing me and making me go crazy for him to hurry up and just lower them out of the damn way.

I'm practically sitting on top of my laptop at this point, licking the damn screen.

His body is even more beautiful than I'd imagined. Every dip of muscles has me aching to run my lips over it.

Sliding his tongue over his bottom lip, he pulls it into his mouth and slides it between his teeth, while lowering his sweats enough to see that he's not wearing anything beneath.

I instantly start fanning myself off, while watching him lower it further down to expose the base of his thick, hard shaft.

"There's not much stopping you from seeing my cock now. It's already hard and waiting for you to tell me what to do with it."

"Oh my fucking . . . oh shit. I'm about to see my boss' dick. This is against all the fucking rules, but I want it so bad."

> BadGirl@heart ~ *Take your sweats off. I want to see you touch your dick for me.*

I can't believe I'm doing this or that I just said that to him.

Smiling big now, he turns the other way and lets his sweats lower to his feet, giving me a full on view of his very sexy, muscular ass.

I see him move his legs, stepping out of his sweats, before he kicks them aside. Then he squirts something in his hand and his arms move as if he's stroking himself. His muscles flex and so do mine as I watch him.

"Hope you're naked by this point. If not . . ." he lets out a husky laugh. "You're going to want to be."

Feeling my pussy lightly clench from his words, I realize that I've never been so damn horny in my entire life.

I'm so turned on right now that it almost hurts. This has never happened. My toes are on fire with the heat that is spreading down my body.

Watching his ass as he slowly strokes his dick, I spread my legs and slide a finger inside my panties, surprised at how wet and slick I am down there.

BadGirl@heart ~ I'm ready . . .

"I hope you're fucking ready, because I'm so damn horny right now that I can't wait to come for you."

Turning around, he slowly runs his hand over his enormous length a few times, before releasing it, giving me a chance to take it all in. He moves it from side to side a few times, allowing me to see that it extends past his leg like he's showing off and I appreciate the show. He's standing there with such confidence while he manages to twist me so tight.

"Holy fuck!" My finger works faster, pushing in and out as my eyes stay glued to his dick, taking in every last detail.

The head is smooth and the shaft is long and thick—so damn hard that the veins are throbbing as he grabs it again and begins stroking.

There's really no other way to describe it other than it's the biggest, most beautiful dick I've ever seen and I want it on me and inside of me.

I never thought I'd say that. Ever.

Just when I thought I'd seen everything I need to have memories to keep me up for a lifetime, he adds to it. The sound of him literally slapping his palm with his dick proves how hard he is. The repetitive hard slapping noises do something to my insides and I can't even comprehend how hot this is. *Does he have any idea how fucking sexy he is?*

I stop to lean forward long enough to get a closer look of what I'm seeing. With my mouth wide open and my eyes focused on his gorgeous cock, I sit back down and resume my position of pleasuring myself.

His strokes speed up then slow to a torturous rhythm while he rubs his thumb over the head a few times. He's standing close to the screen now and I can't see his face. His dick is so close to the screen, I can see every bit of the moisture leaking from the tip. He's lubing himself up even more with each stroke using the pre-come that's dripping out.

Seeing him getting close to coming for me has me so close to release that I'm literally moaning and biting my bottom lip so hard that I may have just drawn blood.

"Fuck me . . ." Slowing down, he grips his dick harder and leans his head back, drawing out his release as it squirts out hard and fast, coating his hand.

He continues to stroke it, covering his dick with his release as he moans out.

I whimper out myself, losing control as my own orgasm rocks through me, almost causing me to scream out because it feels so damn good.

My mouth is frozen in an O of enjoyment, when I look up to see his face in the screen as if he's watching me. His smile is gorgeous and I wish like hell he was really looking at me like that and not some blank screen.

I slide my fingers out of my panties, dragging the moisture over my cleavage before I lean my elbow on the desk to appreciate his face just a few minutes longer. I can't believe this just happened. I have a feeling he'd be livid if he had any idea one of his new employees was on the other end of this call.

Reaching for a Kleenex, I lean over my laptop and end up spilling my water all over the keyboard. In a panic, I start cussing and lift it from the table hoping to keep most of the water from settling. I don't want my last few minutes to end, so I set it down and reach to start drying some of the spill only to practically have a heart attack when I see the damn camera button flashing green.

"Oh shit!" Freaking out, I quickly slam the computer closed and fight to catch my breath.

Not only from the most intense orgasm of my life, but from the fact that my boss might have just seen my face and now knows that I asked him to touch himself for me, knowing that it was him the whole time. I can't believe I was so clumsy. What in the hell? *Maybe he didn't see me.*

I'm going to kill Remi for not telling me these guys are local. No wonder there was so many drop dead gorgeous guys in the club last night and I even thought I recognized a couple of the faces.

This is not good. So not good.

Although nothing has ever felt better in my entire life.

My boss is the beautiful dicked man that every girl fantasizes about and now I want him. So damn bad . . .

Chapter SIX

Lynx

HOLY SHIT. I'M EITHER SEVERELY fucked up about the new bartender, or that comical display of craziness was *her* after she got to see her boss in action.

I was just about to spend a few minutes messaging *BadGirl@ heart* since she was a new client, then all of a sudden the screen came alive with chaos, and in the midst of all that, I swear it was *her* tits and tats that the camera was focused on once the screen stopped moving.

Her long, thick brown hair was there . . . the girl was built like her, with some tattoos that were a blur as she moved, but I didn't get a clear shot of the face. *Fuck.*

I'll just have to torment her a little to see if it was really her. I'm guessing I'll be able to tell the second she sees me. I can always tell when a woman has watched me. She's either blushing or attached to me like she's in heat. I have to say I prefer the blushing type over the aggressive horny ones.

I mean shit, a guy needs a little challenge once in a while and there aren't many women out there willing to give one. Especially in this fucking line of business.

I'm not the slightest pissed that one of my employees might've just seen me, I'm more frustrated with the thought that it was actually her and I didn't have the chance to thoroughly introduce myself as the entertainer I'm known to be. That was a shitty show and since it was my last one for the night, I made sure I came so I wouldn't go to bed with my balls hurting.

"Fuck." I exhale loudly as I finally take my eyes away from the black screen. Why couldn't I break the fucking rules and record the people on the other end? Then there'd be no question because I would've watched the damn recording in slow motion just to know if it was her or not.

Hell, it was *her* body in my mind when I came. It was her fucking sexy body in my mind all damn night.

My schedule is all fucked up since I bought *Club Royal* and to say I've been stressed is a fucking understatement. I need some shit to give soon or I'm going to sell that fucking place just for the mere fact that I don't have time to deal with personnel issues.

"You ready?" Blaze busts in and I want to kick his damn ass for never knocking. I hope like hell one day he walks in to find me balls deep inside some girl and then maybe he'll consider knocking.

Knowing him, he'd try to join in and I'd have to keep from killing him just to finish the job.

"Five grand for thirty minutes. Get your ass up and let's make this happen." He begins pacing like he's fucking nervous and I can't help but wonder what the hell is up with him.

"What's the request?"

"She wants you and Knox in the room with me."

"No fucking way. I'm not fucking sword fighting dicks to get money when I'm bringing in the money I do on the damn daily. Get one of the other guys," I say firmly. "Levi will have no problem."

"No can do. She wants you."

"Well, she can want in one hand and finger herself with the other. I'm not going in."

"You know this is a whole new direction for the company now that we're all in the same house. I'd think you'd want to see how the shit works out before we start offering special shows like this," he points out.

"I'm not so sure this is a direction I'll take the house."

"You'd be an idiot then. She's ready to drop five fucking grand to watch three of us for half an hour." He continues to stand over me until I rise to my feet and contemplate his idea. Maybe he does have a point there.

"Blaze. We have to have fucking boundaries and rules in place before we go into something like that. I'm not running a live fuck feed and these people will start to request shit that most of us aren't going to do. Then we piss off customers because shit isn't ironed out in the beginning. We need to meet on this as a house and decide if we'll do any combo shows. Then offer it on the site as an option. I'm not going in to some fucking room and winging it with two naked guys for thirty minutes. You can fuck off."

"Give it fifteen then. I'll go in and tell her we'll do three grand for fifteen." He's a fucking persistent little fuck when he wants something bad enough.

Shit.

"You're such a pain in the ass."

"But I make you some major fucking money, Brother. You know I'm right about this. Let me help take the club to a whole new level."

I sit back in my chair and think about what he's saying. Fifteen minutes is nothing and it's a perfect time for me to test it out and see how this might go down. I can consider this my one and only combo session unless a miracle happens and something changes my mind.

"Fine. But touch me with your dick and I'll yank that fucker off your body," I growl.

"Calm down. The last thing I want to be near is your dick, but I'm willing to be in the same room for that kind of cash."

"Alright. Go get Knox on board. I have just a few things to do to close up my night in here. Tell her we'll do her call at one." I hear him close the door just as I sit back in front of the black screen on my computer.

I have a few last minute emails to send tonight. The grand opening party is tomorrow night and I've only invited three of my clients. We were supposed to get at least ten a piece in here. Hell, I may have to roam the streets to get my invites in here.

The profile of BadGirl@heart stares back at me and the curiosity is killing me. Is it the hot Miss Rebel that has been haunting my thoughts, or just some woman that had a few similarities?

Who knows. Honestly I haven't been myself since the guys moved in and *Club Royal* started to take over more of my time than I wanted.

I doubt she'd come to the party if it is her, so I find it easy to hit send on the invite headed to her email. I do however get a feeling of satisfaction knowing that I'm teasing the hell out of her if it is her.

Thinking about her reaction to receiving the email forces a giant smile on my face before I move on to send a few more emails.

> ### Private Invitation
>
> You're invited to a special grand opening party this Saturday night at the Alphachat.com mansion. All identities will remain private at this glow in the dark event as we spend time with some of our favorite clients. This invitation is good only for the owner of this profile. You'll receive special instructions for the event once you confirm your acceptance to this invitation.
>
> We look forward to this event and hope you'll be in attendance.
>
> Sincerely,
> Your guys in the Alpha House

Honestly, if it is her I won't want nine other women here to meet me. She'll be my focus and that may piss some of my clients off. So I really need to think about how I want to handle this.

I spend the next hour doing paperwork and finalizing a few emails that I needed to send.

"Hey, Boss. I'm back. Let me know if you have any extra calls to handle tonight. I cleared all of mine to handle the club." Nash stands in the doorway to my room looking at me and I feel guilty that he dealt with the club tonight for me and lost out on so much potential money in his own pocket. That fucking club may be the death of me.

"Nash. I'll cover your fees for the calls you missed tonight. Thank you for taking care of the club."

"No worries," he says smoothly in his Southern accent. "I actually enjoyed the change of pace. It's nice to have conversations with real legit women standing in front of me while I work. I'm not gonna lie. Some of those tits in that club do wonders for stored images for this job." We both laugh as he walks a few feet into my room.

"I hear ya. Do you have all of your invitations out for the party tomorrow night?"

"Sure do. All of mine confirmed earlier this week. Most of mine are flying in."

"Good deal." This is the exact reason I decided to have this party. My new guys all need exposure and I think this will be a great way to get them that. It doesn't bother me one bit if I don't end up with a single client of my own in the house.

Hell . . . the truth is, they're all my clients.

"Alright. Well if you don't mind, I'm heading out for a while."

"See you tomorrow," I say with a single nod.

I have to respect that guy. Not many of them would've checked in here before they went out. I need to make sure I take care of that one. It wouldn't hurt them all to take notes from him.

"Alright, Asshole. It's go time." Blaze steps around Nash as he leaves and I glance down at my watch. It is about that time and now I wish like hell I had never told him I'd do this shit.

"Give me a few seconds to get going, I'll be right there."

"She wants us commando in jeans!" he yells at me from behind the door after he closes himself out.

I slide my jeans off and then my briefs. Standing here naked in my quiet room, I try to decide how the hell this is all going to go.

I dip my hand into my coconut oil and start to slowly stroke my cock to the image frozen on the big screen above.

This is a normal nightly ritual for me to get started on my night. I'm not usually starting it all again so quickly right after I let myself come on the last call. Very few get the money shot. That new client has no idea how lucky she was to get that kind of show from me on a first call and she sure as hell is lucky to have received it on a fifteen minute one.

Fuck. I start to think about the odds that it was her behind that screen, just as a reply comes in from her invitation, drawing my attention to my email.

She accepted the invite.

Hell yes.

Now I'll make sure she doesn't leave here without her own personal one on one time with me and me alone. The other guys better keep their dicks aimed somewhere else.

It takes me no time to get hard thinking about her now. Fuck the tits frozen on the big screen. The ones I glimpsed on my computer were pure fucking perfection.

I slide my jeans back on my hips, guiding my dick across my left upper thigh before zipping them up. My bulge is obvious as I open the door to Blaze's room to find Knox already starting his teasing for the client.

The screen is black, but she's allowing us to listen to her. Her heavy breathing into the monitor proves she likes what she sees when it comes to Knox and what he calls his *Southern charmer*. Hell, I don't doubt that his dick probably has more charm than most of the guys in this house.

"I see my three favorite men are all finally together. I was beginning to think I'd have to pay the Alpha House a visit myself just to get this done." Her voice is sensual and very breathy, showing us just how worked up she already is.

I stand in the background and work to think about Rebel

again. She's done the job for me the past few rounds, so why not try to see if she can get me through this nightmare.

"Alright, Big Guy. Jeans off. Move slow and tease me just like I like it, Lynx." I recognize the profile as I move closer.

Cougar69 is one of our very loyal clients. I sent her to Blaze when she got frustrated that I couldn't fit her into my schedule enough for her liking. I can do this for this woman. Hell, I owe a lot of my success to her.

I unzip my jeans before I lift my cock out of them and into her view. "Hell yes. You three are my fantasy," she says with a small moan. "I just wish I could talk you into a show like this in person." I ignore her insinuated request and continue working my already coconut oil moistened cock. "Now in that deep sexy voice of yours, tell me what *your* fantasy is," she requests, seductively.

I start to give her the standard reply I always have to this type of question, where a woman rides me when I'm driving down the road, when my mind diverts back to a certain beautiful woman: *Rebel*.

"I see a gorgeous woman covered in sweat standing against a bar." I pause and allow my memories to replay a scene I wish I could go back and redo. "She looks over at me while she runs her fingers over her damp glistening cleavage telling me how hot it is." I continue to stroke my dick while I finish the fantasy in my head, but only say pieces of it out loud. "She slides her fingers under her dress showing off a perfectly curved ass before her fingers disappear inside her."

"Damn, Lynx. Stop talking before I come from your words alone." She's practically panting before she asks for Blaze to join in.

Knox and I stand in the background and continue stroking while she talks to him. He drops his jeans to his ankles and I look for something else to focus on. Blaze's ass isn't going to do it for me.

"Alright boys. I want all three of you in view. Front and center." We move forward and stand close enough to give her a view of all three of our cocks. I don't look down, instead look to Blaze to give him an idea of how bad I'm going to kill him after this shit is over.

He smiles and starts talking to the cougar until she's moaning her dramatic release through the high quality speakers in Blaze's room.

I hold my dick in my hand and give her a stroke show through the process, but this scene didn't win her a damn money shot, even with picturing the hot as fuck woman that's been fucking with my head all night.

This is so fucked up.

Chapter SEVEN

Rebel

"SHIT. I'M DYING, REMI. HE has to know it was me. What am I going to do?"

"You're going to act like you liked the show, dammit. I don't see what the big deal is. If he wanted to hide it, he shouldn't show his face when he has a session." She's still in bed, even though I've been screaming through this house since I slammed my laptop closed.

"How do you expect me to act normal after what I just saw? He's freaking gorgeous under his clothes. Hell, he's difficult enough to work around knowing what he looks like *with* his clothes on, now I have to pretend I didn't just see what I saw." I plop on the end of her bed and purposely block her view so she'll listen to me and stop watching TV.

"What exactly did you see, Rebel? I still can't believe Lynx is your damn boss. Tell me you fingered yourself through his show."

"I know and what? No, I'm not telling you that." I stand to leave on that note. She's obviously not seeing this as the emergency that I do, so this is a hopeless mess I've gotten myself into.

"I'm going to bed and never coming out of my room again. It was nice knowing you."

I hold my head in embarrassment all the way back to my room. I can't believe I let her talk me into a sex chat. It's my own fault, I should've known it would be a disaster and it was.

A. Total. Fucking. Disaster.

My laptop has to be seriously fried now on top of the disaster and embarrassment. Not a good way to end the night at all.

I tip it over a towel and let the remainder of the extra water drip out, praying that it will still work. I'm not sure my face could frown any harder as I open it slowly.

I stand to the side just in case he's still able to see, through the slim chance that it's still working and he's still connected. I know that won't happen, but I'm taking extra precautions to prevent even the slightest possibility.

I power it on and it seems to be working. "Oh thank God." This is one of those moments I'm glad I always spend good money on a quality computer.

After letting the page load back up, a ding notifies me of a message within the Alphachat.com site. I grab my heart in panic, the second I see the subject. My scream is out long before I even consider the ramifications of being loud with something like this on my computer.

Remi comes barreling into the room and looks at me with an unsureness. It may have something to do with the fact that I'm standing across the room pointing at the computer like a monster is literally coming through it. She slowly walks toward it and I don't move a muscle as she bends over to read it.

"You, Bitch. I was hoping to get one of these. Holy shit! It's a glow in the dark party. How fucking cool would that be?" She turns to look at me while I'm still frozen in time and speechless.

"Well you have to go."

"No fucking way. He'll know it's me."

"He probably already knows that. Who knows maybe that's why you got the invite so quickly. I mean shit, you're a first timer. I should have a room in that house of theirs with the amount of money I've spent in the past few months."

"Remi. I can't. That's not my scene."

"No, it isn't. Your fucking scene is this room in front of this computer . . . Whyyyy the fuck is your keyboard wet? Tell me you're not one of those squirting bitches and I just touched your lady come."

"Oh my god, Remi. No. It's water." I finally take a step toward the computer and begin to let my eyes refocus on the exact wording. Just as I do, she slides her finger over the mouse pad and taps on the word 'accept'.

"What did you dooooo? Undo. Undo. Undo. Remi what the hell?" She stands as I continue to panic, hitting random buttons.

"Oh, calm down. You'll thank my ass tomorrow night," she gloats.

"Tomorrow. Holy shit. I'm not going. I'll just not even leave the house the entire day."

"You will. There's no way I'm letting you get one of those damn invites and not attend. That's just not even fair to all of us horny women who've been hoping to be one of the lucky chosen few." I listen to her as she walks to her bedroom, yelling at me the whole way. "You're going and it's final!"

I lay back on my bed and try to calm the chaos in my head. Replaying our chat session, I try to remember if I ever touched the screen before the water fell. If not, maybe he didn't see me. If I did. Well, then he saw a *lot* of me.

I've never even been to a glow in the dark party. What do you even wear to something like that? It doesn't matter. I can't entertain this idea. The awkwardness of him realizing that it was me if he didn't already know would be horrible.

He'd be furious. I've seen him angry and that would be embarrassing if he decided to make a point with me. I can only imagine he doesn't want his employees from the club mixing with the guys of the house, let alone with him specifically.

What is happening? This can't be happening. I'll wake up soon and all of this will be over.

I close my eyes and try to pretend this didn't happen. The panic in my chest tells me that I'm very much awake and that it isn't just a bad dream no matter how much I wish it was.

THAT MIGHT'VE OFFICIALLY BEEN THE worst night's rest of my life. I can't even deal with the thought of going tonight. It kept my mind occupied all night with scenarios. Some good . . . some bad. Very bad, which somehow made them good. If that even makes sense.

Hell, I don't even know.

The sound of my regular emails coming in, keeps me from trying to force myself back to sleep and going near the computer right now isn't an option. I'm thinking if I stay in bed 'til at least ten this morning, it'll all seem better. I don't want to move or even think yet.

My laptop makes a very different sound causing me to jump up from my bed and creep closer. I get within view of the screen and see a missed message from Lynx Kade, the gorgeous chatroom entertainer.

Not to be confused with Lynx Kade, my boss.

> *Lynx: I'm looking forward to seeing you tonight. There are only a few house rules for the glow in the dark party. You must wear a bathing suit, because the only thing glowing will be the*

paint you add to your body when you first arrive. There will be a room with very talented artists designing whatever you wish. Lights will go out at 8pm and will not be turned back on until dawn. You're one of three that I've invited, so don't let me down.

Body paint? *Why does that sound insanely sexy? 'Don't let me down.' Really?* I like knowing that he won't be able to see me fully. Maybe he won't be able to tell it's me. Who am I kidding, he probably doesn't even remember me anyway. I'm just one of the many women he has been in the same room with.

I close the message without responding. This isn't something I'll be able to pull off. I should just send Remi to the party, she's the one that wanted to go anyway.

Moving slower than usual, I go into the kitchen to make some coffee. Remi looks about like I do as she saunters into the room, looking mostly still asleep. "Did you hear from the Alpha?" she asks with a cocked eyebrow.

"Yeah."

"What do you mean, yeah? You can't just say that and not explain." She's awake now. Her face has brightened up and I can tell this day is going to be a giant pain in my ass. Especially since Remi has the day off, giving her a whole lot of hours to bug me about tonight.

"It was just instructions to that party that I'm not attending," I say casually, as if it's the furthest thing from my mind.

"Can I ask why you're being dumb this morning?" She huffs. "Should I remind you of the cobwebs building up inside that unused vag of yours?"

"Ew. What's wrong with you?" My face scrunches up in disgust at the image now in my head. It's too early for this.

"Just trying to remind you that you need to take every chance you can to get some action," she says without even a hint of shame.

"I'm working at the top club in the city now, what more do you want from me?" I ask with a small yawn.

"Nothing. Except for you to go to this party."

"It's my boss, Remi. Do you not understand that?"

"Oh, I understand perfectly. How fucking hot is that? He invited you, so you must go."

"I don't even have a bathing suit." I point out.

"Ok, hold on crazy. Why do you need one of those?"

"Because that's what his instructions were this morning. Wear a bathing suit and artists will be there to add glow in the dark paint to my body."

"Holy fucking hell, I hate you right now." She stands and continues yelling at me again from her room, then back to the kitchen. "How is it that shy Rebel is invited to something like this, while the bold one, will be here fighting off some giant asshole date again?" She plops her butt on the stool in front of me. "Here. You'll thank me with that blue one." She throws a handful of bathing suits on the counter and colorful strings splay out all around me.

"I'm not going," I mutter.

"Yes, you are."

"Are you going to harass me until I do?"

Please say no. Please say no . . .

"You're damn right I am. This is a once in a lifetime opportunity and you're going to go and then tell me all about it," she says with finality.

"Do you at least have a cover up?" I ask on a sigh, feeling more and more helpless as the conversation goes on.

"Nope. You won't need one."

"You're evil."

"You know you love me."

She's right about the love thing. Not so sure about this party though. I take a deep breath and then a drink of coffee before I just take the plunge and agree to go.

"Fine. I'll go." *I'm insane. Definitely insane.*

"YES! I'll help you with your makeup and hair."

She screams the yes before she starts making plans to make me beautiful. I just sip my coffee and let her talk. I know her well enough to know this is something that she will want to be a part of, even though it's going to be dark. I know not to ask her why we're doing all this if it'll be dark. She'd just say something ridiculous about me being there 'til morning.

"Put on the blue one so I can see how your tits and ass look."

"You're barbaric. It'll be fine." I walk to my room with the intention of trying it all on by myself, but she follows.

"No, you really need to try the bikini on. Your tits are kind of ginormous compared to mine." She lifts a brow at my tits. "Seriously . . . it's not even fair."

"Alright, alright. Give me a second and then I'll let you in." I close the door and lock it because I don't trust her. I also want the option to not let her see me in it if I feel that's what needs to happen.

I tie it on and catch myself in the mirror. "Holy shit, I can't wear this."

"Why? Let me see." I open the door and her eyes bulge when she zones in on my cleavage. "Perfect! Now show me that ass." She walks around me and continues to analyze me even though I'm doing everything I can to cover myself with my arms.

"Stop that. Stand proud. You're gorgeous, Rebel. This is perfect!" I turn a few times in the mirror and try to stop the critical thoughts running through my mind. "He's going to be all over you! Make sure they paint you in a way that accentuates these assets, girl." She points at each of my boobs then at my ass again.

I should feel better about going, but I don't. She has to say these things. She's my friend and we all know how that is.

༅

WE SHOPPED FOR FIVE HOURS. Four hours too long, if you ask me. I managed to get my hair and nails done before we looked everywhere for the perfect heels. That probably took the longest, since in her opinion, they had to be the sexiest ones on the market.

Now I'm in Remi's car on my way to this mansion, she's just dying to get behind the gates of herself, fighting my damn nerves and trying not to look so uptight. She insisted that she drive me so I can drink tonight and loosen up. I think this is her way of making sure I don't leave the party too early. She's smart.

"I'll be right by the phone. If you find out you can actually bring a friend, you call me. Oh and also, I guess you can call me when you're ready to go." I smile at her humor.

I wish like everything that she could go inside with me. This night would be so much easier if she could. Or maybe it wouldn't. She'd probably force me into something crazy that I'd regret later.

"Thanks, Remi," I say, while shaking out my nerves. "I'll call you in a few hours. You make sure you're listening. Got it."

"Why don't you not call me! Have a good time, Rebel!" She rolls down the window to tell me goodbye and I take a moment to feel the night air on my mostly naked skin. It has my whole body tingling with goose bumps.

I wore a sundress over the bathing suit; it just felt better like that, rather than the other option of showing up half-naked in a pair of six inch heels.

It's already almost dark outside, but it's obvious where I'm supposed to enter. The strobe lights in front of an otherwise dark mansion should be my first clue.

I walk until an overly excited woman pulls me aside and offers to paint anything I want on my body. I wish I would've talked this over with Remi, because right now my mind is blank.

I finally just tell her to paint me how ever she wants to. She seems happy about this, smiling as she asks my profile name, then begins to paint it up the side of my thigh.

She then moves me behind a dark screen and asks me to remove my top and bottoms.

"Why would I have to do that?" I ask, sounding more panicked than I was hoping to let on.

"Because you're one of Lynx's invites," she replies. "I was asked to make sure to paint you nude then add the bathing suit over the top.

I hesitate for a few minutes and wish like hell I hadn't let Remi talk me into this. How can I let someone paint me naked? And why is he the only one requesting that?

What have I done? I think I'm in way over my head.

Chapter EIGHT

Lynx

THIS PLACE IS PACKED. GLOW in the dark female bodies are everywhere. Most of the guys haven't made their way out yet, and I'm sitting here in my office in the dark with my clothes on. I purposely made my office overlook the main room just so I could watch on nights like this.

I'm trying to decide if I'll be joining the party tonight at all. I only ended up sending an invite to three of my clients. My late night messaging was interrupted and I forgot to get back in there to send a few more. Not that it really matters anyway. There's only one I was determined to get here.

I'm really only down here to see if *BadGirl@heart* shows up. My mind can't get over the chance that it might just be Rebel from the club. I guess you could say she's been fucking with my head for almost a week now, so I guess I hope it is her.

I'm thinking a good actual fuck tonight from one of these girls will pull me out of that funk if she doesn't actually show up. I just need to decide which one I'll let in my room.

This house changes dramatically with the feel of females in the air. I can smell their perfume and the air just feels different.

Watching a few more of the girls enter, I continue to drink my whiskey before I tip the bottle over the glass and refill it. This little bar is hidden out of view right inside my office and I think it's the perfect place for me to just sit back and watch.

We've lined all of the furniture and doorways in the house with a special glow tape. I know the clean-up for this party will be horrendous, but I plan to hire someone to get it done. As it is I've had to hire a crew to come in here daily to make sure it stays decent. I forgot how filthy guys are to live with. Not to mention they all have crazy hours to keep up with, but I can't complain because that means money in my pocket.

I'm stopped mid thought when I see the words *BadGirl@heart* glowing down the right thigh of the female coming through the front door.

I study her. The damn darkness is hiding so much of her, but I have to admit that I'm loving the paint on her body. I told the artists to paint my three women in the nude. It's a special treat for my girls that no others will receive. I guess you could say I was planning to fuck one of them, and I'd like to knock this off my bucket list.

Watching the female body move as it glows in the dark will be a great turn on for me. I'm somewhat of a voyeur and I can't hide from that. In fact, it's what my business is focused around.

Her paint is flawless, just like her body. Her paint resembles a long blue evening dress that glows down her entire body. The front of the dress is painted so that it looks like it's open between her tits and all the way down to her mid stomach, then back open all the way down her right leg.

She turns around to take in the room and I get to see the entire canvas. Her back is painted to look like she's wearing one of those dresses you have to lace up. I'm wondering how long she was in the paint room, because the detail on this is immaculate.

She's by far the most covered in paint and I make a mental note to give the artist responsible for this one hell of a tip.

Her tits are fucking perfect. The paint outlines her curves and I'm left licking my lips, dying to get close to her. She only has her face painted around her eyes; her lids glow, leaving me to crave a look into her eyes.

She begins to look around the room in a rush, and if I'm not mistaken, she's about to bolt. I stand and leave my office to walk toward her, dodging a few females on my path. My darkness allows me to approach her without her even knowing that I'm near. I walk around the edge of the room and stand in front of the exit door to watch her.

She slides her hands down her arms, then crosses her arms over her chest. She's standing there so innocently, causing my dick to twitch. *Fuck.* I don't care who this *BadGirl@heart* is. I will be doing whatever I have to do to get her into my bed tonight.

She starts walking toward me with her head tilted down. I stand solid and allow her to walk straight into my body before I hold my hands out to guide her even closer.

"Where are you going?" I speak in her ear over the music playing throughout the house.

"Oh, I'm so sorry I didn't see you there. I'm going home." She's nervous and afraid to look up at me. It's one hundred percent Rebel from the club and now I find her to be even more of a challenge to me. I think I'll keep it a secret that I know it's her for at least a little while.

"So soon?" I slide my hands up her arms, feeling her soft skin the whole way up. "Such a shame. After I had the artist spend so much time on this gorgeous body."

Her laughter surprises me. "How many times have you said that tonight?"

"You're actually the first woman I've said a word to," I admit.

"Oh. Well, sorry. I'm not sure why I even came. I just thought the party sounded unique."

"Everything I do is unique." She finally looks up at me, searching in the darkness to see my face, and I can finally see the true art around her eyes. Her lids look like butterfly wings and the paint around them finishes the beauty of the entire image.

"Well, that's a great quality to have." She steps back from me just slightly. "Thank you for the invitation. Have a great night." She walks toward the hall marked restroom while I stand there in complete shock that she just brushed me off.

I'm Lynx fucking Kade. I don't get brushed off. In fact, I have a waiting list of females who want to have their chance with me. I have to admit, I'm turned on even more now.

I follow her closely and let the energy of her little game fuel me. She opens the bathroom door, before I grab the knob behind her, pulling it closed with both of us inside. Turning the lock, I ensure that we won't be interrupted by anyone walking in on us.

"Tell me you're not here to feel what Lynx Kade feels like." She stands speechless while I run my fingers over both of her hardened nipples. "I know I'm dying to see the full painting on this sexy canvas." I slide my hand around her neck and pull one of the strings, allowing her bikini top to fall.

We both inhale sharply as it hits the floor after I tug on the second string behind her back. *Holy fuck.* Her tits are gorgeous and very visible. Her whole body is glowing in this otherwise dark room and my dick is so fucking hard right now.

My fingers itch to touch her nipples again, so I do and she doesn't pull away from me. I listen to her breathing and know I have her full approval so far. It's quite a change from the woman that tried to leave the party only a few minutes ago. Something seems to be keeping her in here with me. Perhaps she wants me just as badly as I want her. She may not know that I know who she is, but I know for damn sure that she knows I'm her boss.

"Are you still leaving my party?"

"I really should," she breathes softly.

"Or you could stay. I'm thinking we could think of something that would entertain you enough to convince you to stay." I let my fingers slide around the outline of the paint on her body.

"I'm sure you could."

"Come to my room with me." She takes a deep breath, no doubt thinking about her choices. I don't like how long she's taking, so I lower my lips to hers and try to do a little convincing.

Her lips are soft and her kiss is sensual and slow. I'd give anything to bite her lip right now and not scare the shit out of her, but something tells me it would make her run.

"I really should go."

Yep, she would run.

"You should at least have a drink with me." She's quiet for a few seconds while I watch her tits rise and fall with each breath. "It's the least you can do if you plan to leave me so early, *BadGirl@heart*. I sent you a special invitation." I make it a point to call her by her screenname and not her real name.

This little game she's playing is hot as fuck.

"I can have one drink with you."

"Alright, but we have to do it my way." I hand her back her bikini top and even tie it for her from behind. My eyes never leave the mirror as I catch her glow moving in the dark.

"What did I get myself into?" she says quietly as I open the door before I lead her back to my office.

I can see the guys have made their way to the main floor, so I won't be missed back here.

"What's your drink of choice?" I have to ask because I know a bartender will have a preference.

"I'll let you choose." I can see the glow in her upper cheeks lift, so I know she's smiling about this. I wish to fuck I wouldn't have done this whole dark thing so I could actually see her, but this is sexy and mysterious.

"Drop 'em." She stays quiet until I say it again. "Drop 'em."

"Drop what?"

"Your bikini top and bottoms."

"You're out of your mind." I lift my shirt to expose the few painted lines that are visible beneath my jeans. Even in the dark, I can tell her eyes have lowered to see where those glow lines lead.

"Alright. I won't drop mine either then." I let my shirt fall again.

She places her hand on my wrist and holds it while she battles with her next sentence.

"Tell me exactly what you're planning to do here, first."

"Well, I plan to have a tequila shot off of your body. I'm thinking you can hold it between your legs for me then I'll need a chaser, so I'll kiss you." She lets go of my wrist and reaches behind her neck to untie the strings.

"How about just the top. Then I get to do a body shot off of you."

Fuck yes you do.

"Yes. I can work with that."

"Well then, I guess I should tell you to drop 'em too," she says, sounding a bit more relaxed now.

I toss my shirt on the bar and my jeans at my ankles. My dick is glowing and pretty much standing at full attention. I give her a little visual of how big it is by moving it across the width of my thigh. That's a true measure of length.

Hardness is proven the second I slam it against my palm, echoing a hammer like sound through the little bar area even with the music playing.

"Holy shit," she whispers, making my mouth turn up into a

smile.

"Who's first?" I ask. In this situation I can't lose. I'm either putting my lips on her or she's putting hers on me.

"Um. I'll let you show me how it's done."

Music to my ears. My only hope is she follows my lead on this.

"Lay back and hold this between your legs." I lift her so that she's sitting on the end of the bar and her legs dangle down the side. I set the glow in the dark shot glass in the dark little spot between her legs and fight off the urge to let my fingers explore while I'm down here. She fidgets until it's set in position and I reach for the Patron.

Before I begin to pour, I close the doors to my office and stand back to observe the scene in front of me. The sexy glow from her body is tormenting me and my dick is begging to play.

I pour slowly, purposely spilling it a little over the edge of the rim. She squirms with the spill and I move to slow her nerves about this, by talking to her, allowing my face to be right above hers as I do.

"You are so fucking sexy right now. You come in here looking like pure innocence and all I want to do is pull sin straight from your body." I lean down to kiss her lips again just to test her acceptance of me. Shit, it's hard to do all this in pitch black darkness.

She kisses me back, slowly at first but then she matches my intensity so I kiss her a little longer than I planned. She's a great kisser. Her tongue has me thinking about what she'd be like with it around my cock.

I'm fucking glad I made sure this paint is safe to consume. I had a feeling a few people might need that as an option.

I let my tongue slide down her body, outlining the painted dress the entire way. Stepping to the end of the bar, I slide her to the edge and lean over her to place my mouth over the glass. I can see her hands gripping the edge of the bar on both sides like she's hanging on for her life. I'm just now noticing the tiny painted lines down each of her fingers.

Without using my hands, I put my mouth over the rim and tip the glass back. I quickly slide her legs further apart and untie the strings at her hips, giving me access to my chaser. Before she has a chance to resist, I place my mouth over her and let my tongue do all the work.

She tries to resist for about a half second before she's opening her legs even wider for me. I kiss her aggressively while I take in every squirm she makes. It's sweet. So fucking sweet, like damn candy.

I want to take her to the edge, but not over because it'll keep her here. This woman has to be in my bed tonight or I'm going to have to go on a fuck spree just to get my cock to settle the hell down.

Sliding her even further past the edge of the bar, I hold her hips in the air and continue to fuck her with my tongue. She tastes so fucking good and if I had to guess, she used some sort of flavored cream before she came here. A smile brushes across my face as I take in her bold confidence in doing that.

I could definitely handle a woman who likes to surprise a little during play time. Her death grip on the edge of the bar draws my attention, so I pull away, leaving her chest moving rapidly up and down with each breath. She doesn't get to finish this soon.

Playing is my specialty.

Setting her back on her feet, I let her taste herself from my lips. She doesn't shy away from the kiss, but her hands aren't moving to explore any further.

I pull away from her kiss in hopes of moving this to the next level.

"Your turn"

"Uh, ok." I see her turn to scan the mostly dark room. I've had the bar and the chase lounge outlined as well as the floor around my desk. Other than that, it's dark in here.

"Can you lay down over there?" I hand her the tequila and start walking to the brand new lounge chair she points to. It would make me happy as fuck if I could break it in with her tonight.

I quickly grab a lime wedge and lay back where she wants me. She follows my lead, setting the glass between my legs and then gets down on her knees between my legs.

I watch her tits and her eye lids glow as she leans down for the glass. Watching the glow move around so quickly is distracting me, but I'm definitely entertained.

She pulls the glass away from her lips and looks a bit hesitant to make her next move. Knowing that she's going to need a bit of convincing, I squirt a few drops of lime at the base of my dick, not wanting it anywhere near my damn head and grab her hair to guide her up to where I want her.

Her tongue comes out to quickly lick the lime off my dick. Just as she's about to pull away, I grip her hair harder and growl out, letting her know she's not done with her chaser.

My glowing cock disappears in her mouth a few times before she adds in tongue movement. I can feel the draw of her tongue up and down it before she takes me deep one last time. The sound of her short little gag goes right through me and I'm fighting like hell not to guide her head even deeper and fuck her mouth.

Holy fuck this is hot.

Chapter NINE

Rebel

HOLY HELL . . . I CAN'T BELIEVE I'm actually doing this right now. This is extremely daring on my part and completely and utterly hot.

The way he feels in my mouth, so big and hard, has me so wet and turned on that I'm not so sure I can *not* have an orgasm in the next five minutes if things continue on this path.

My boss . . . my demanding, sexy and very sinful boss' most *desired* feature is in my mouth right now, filling it and causing me to gag around its length like a dirty girl.

Everything about this moment makes me feel dirty, but damn if I don't like it. It's been a while since I've felt so free and alive with excitement. Adrenaline is coursing through me like never before.

My plan was to make a quick appearance to make Remi happy and keep her off my ass. I was hoping to not be noticed by any of the guys, especially Lynx.

But when I walked through that door and began to look around the vast space, glowing with tons of female bodies, I was ready to bolt right there and then.

The last place I expected to find myself was here in Lynx's office with my mouth wrapped around him.

But when he touched me, I couldn't resist.

The adrenaline of his strong touch and him tasting me so magically with his tongue, has me on some kind of high, making it hard to rationalize the fact that he's my boss and could possibly find out the next time I see him at the club and fire me.

Or worse; call me out on the fact that I went along with it, knowing it was him all along.

I feel Lynx's grip on my hair tighten again, before he tangles his hands in it to the scalp and moans when I take him as deep as I can, gagging for the second time.

"Oh fuck," he moans out deep and oh so damn sexy, causing heat to shoot to the aching between my legs.

Feeling like I've had my fair share of my chaser, I pull away from his dick and run my arm over my mouth in the darkness.

Sitting here naked—on my knees—has what I've really just done sinking in, now that it's done and over.

"I should go." Bolting to my feet, I rush back over to the small bar and struggle with finding my bathing suit.

It's a little harder to find than I'd like it to be right now.

"Stay," he demands. "There's a game I want to play with you."

Working fast to retie my bikini top, I stop and suck in a small breath, when I feel his body behind me and feel the warmth of his breath along my neck, as he reaches for the strings to finish tying for me. "I don't know," I say, unable to stop my curiosity. "What kind of game do you have in mind?"

I feel his laugh against my exposed skin. "Pool. Across the hall. The winner gets a *special* treat."

"Oh yeah?" I question, overcurious what this special treat is. "What about the loser? Does the loser get anything?"

"There's a little fun leading to the grand prize. Plenty enough to make it worth your stay."

It's still early and a part of me isn't ready to leave this sexy man yet. As long as I'm out of here before the lights turn on, I have a shot at keeping my identity a secret.

He hasn't called me out yet. That has to be a good sign that he's forgotten who I am or just can't tell in the dark. I'll take that as a good sign for now.

"And what about the other two women you invited here tonight? Won't they be looking for you?" I question out of curiosity.

"Let them look," he grumbles next to my ear. "I'm busy having fun with you. My new guys will keep them entertained. They need the exposure more than I do."

After pulling on his jeans, but keeping them undone, he grabs my hand and pulls me through the room and across the hall to where there's a partially glowing pool table.

The balls and the pockets are glowing along with the tips of the cue sticks. Other than that, it's pitch black in here, just like the rest of the rooms.

I release a breath, relieved that it will keep my identity a secret, so I can stay and have a little fun.

The only thing I can see on him are the lines above his jeans and the faint glow of the head of his penis sticking out from them, as he picks up a cue stick and hands it to me, before grabbing one of his own.

This is going to be so distracting.

I'm not going to lie, I'm pretty decent at pool, but knowing that his dick isn't fully covered is going to keep my eyes wanting to go elsewhere.

"Each ball has a foreplay activity assigned. You sink your balls, I get to pleasure you. I sink mine and you get to think up your own ways to torture me." He pauses to rack the balls. "The rougher . . . the better. Ladies first."

Holy shit. This sounds hot. Am I'm really doing this?

"Alright . . ." I walk up and get ready to break. "And what does the winner get?"

"Release."

"You're serious?" I question, a bit nervous, knowing that there's a huge chance that he'll be winning this game.

"That's the whole point of punishment. Only *one* of us gets a happy ending, BadGirl@heart. Let's see how bad you want it."

Feeling up to the challenge, I break the balls, sinking in one solid and two stripes. "Looks like I'm stripes."

"Looks like you are," he says with amusement. "I'd pick your next shot wisely. You have no idea what situation it might get you into."

"Oh crap," I whisper under my breath, while trying to figure out my next move. Only balls: 9, 10, 12, 13 and 15 are left for me to choose from and 10 seems to be my only clear shot.

Taking aim, I shoot and tense up, when the 10 sinks into the pocket.

"Ten . . . good choice." Coming up behind me, he pushes my shoulders, until I'm bent over the pool table with my ass in the air.

I breathe heavily, awaiting his next move.

My hands grip the table as I feel his tongue slowly move up my leg, starting from behind my knee and working its way up to my bikini line.

With his mouth, he pushes the bikini aside and slowly and tortuously slips a finger inside my pussy. "So fucking tight," he growls against me, before he pumps in and out a few times. "Let's see how many fingers I can fit."

I bite my bottom lip and moan as he pulls out and pushes back in, but with two fingers this time.

His fingers are so damn thick.

"Oh fuck . . ." He slowly pumps in and out. "My dick will definitely hurt you. You're gonna feel me for days," I hear him whisper behind me and a jolt of something races through me.

I'm not sure if it's excitement or fear. He thinks he's going to fuck me and to be honest right now in this moment, I'd probably let him. He has me so wrapped up in his every move that I can barely breathe between them.

He keeps pumping in and out, until I feel myself beginning to clamp down on his fingers. That's when he decides it's time to pull his fingers out, leaving me wanting more.

"Oh shit," I breathe, while trying to catch my breath.

"You took that punishment well. I'm impressed with my bad girl." I can see the dark silhouette of him running his hand over his now fully erect dick. "And so fucking turned on. Go again."

Fighting to pull my eyes away from his hardness, I take a shot and miss. A part of me is relieved, not sure that I'd be able to handle another punishment so soon.

I can't tell how he's feeling at the moment, because all I can see is his cue stick on the table ready to take a shot.

He sinks in the number six and my heart speeds up with excitement.

It's up to me to make up his punishment. Whatever I want to do to tease him. The power's in my hands right now.

"Come here," I say as firmly as I can, trying to keep my voice from shaking.

I wait for him to stand in front of me, before I grab his jeans and lower them, while falling to my knees, before him. I work hard not to think about what I'm doing. If I stop and think . . . I'll never be able to continue.

Gripping the shaft of his enormous dick, I lift it up and run my tongue over his balls, before sucking the right one into my mouth and teasing it. I pull down on it and he groans out and grips my hair.

Knowing that he's enjoying it, I tug on it a little harder this time, before releasing it and running my tongue up his sack.

I can tell by the way his legs are tensing that he wants me to go higher and take his dick into my mouth, but I don't. That one will be for later.

Releasing his shaft, I stand up and step away from him. "Looks like it's your turn again."

I can't tell from the darkness, but I'm pretty sure he's smiling right now as he takes his next shot, sinking in the number two ball. "I love my balls being sucked and tugged on, but I love my dick being sucked and tugged more."

He steps out of his jeans completely and kicks them aside.

Smiling, I decide to tease him some more, not fully giving him what he wants. I drop to my knees again and without using my hands, I swirl my tongue around the head of his dick, before flicking it with my tongue.

When I suck just the tip of it into my mouth, it must set him off, because he grabs the back of my head and tries to push it in further. I back away, releasing it with a pop, before he can.

I run my nails down his thick thighs, causing him to growl out with pleasure, before I stand back up and smile in the darkness. "Go. Again."

He takes his time with his next shot, so I'm surprised when he misses it. It's almost as if he did it on purpose. "Go," he demands.

I take my shot, sinking in the number twelve ball. Before I can see him coming, his hands grab me and set me on top of the pool table, causing a few of the balls to move across the table.

My bikini top drops to the table, before he lowers to undo my bottoms, pulling me to the edge of the table.

His erection presses against the inside of my thigh, so close to my entrance that I throw my head back and grip the table, dying with everything in me for it to touch me where I need it.

Teasing me, he thrusts his hips a little, rubbing it up the inside of my thigh, but never touching me where I want it the most. It's so fucking close that I can taste it.

With force, he flips me over again so that my stomach is on the table, with my ass hanging over the side for him.

My guess is that he wanted to let me see his beautiful fucking erection, before he does whatever it is he's about to do with it next. He wanted to tease me and it worked.

He grabs my right leg and lifts it up until my knee is pressed against the side of the table, my pussy spread out for him to do whatever he wants with it. Easy access.

I'm almost worried that he's going to slam his enormous dick inside of me, but then that would defeat the purpose of the game. I'd come within five thrusts, getting my release, before we can even determine a winner.

I'm that close to the edge.

I bite my bottom lip when I feel his dick come down on my ass cheek, slapping it hard. Then he does it again. Again. And Again. Until it begins to sting.

He slaps it so close to my aching pussy, that I moan out my pleasure, bringing it to his attention, that he better stop before he makes me come undone too soon.

He now grips my hips, pulling me closer to him, until his erection is resting on my lower back. "Have you had enough," he whispers next to my ear.

I shake my head and what comes out of my mouth next, surprises even me. "No. Keep going."

He gently grips the back of my hair and pulls my head back to whisper in my ear again, "If I keep going we'll both come.

Very fucking hard."

He slaps his dick against my sore ass one more time, before backing away and helping me back up to my feet. His hand strokes up and down his shaft a few times, before he growls out and releases it. "Go."

We're both fully naked now and just knowing that makes me tremble, thinking about what could happen. He's full of surprises and has me intrigued beyond any level I've ever felt before. I can tell he doesn't lead a boring life and I'm sure he'd be irritated to know just how boring I am in mine. It's a good thing I'm living outside of my shell tonight.

I lean across the table and shoot, barely missing the pocket because he begins to distract me. I can see the paint from his cock smearing in his palm as he strokes it just over the top of the table as I aim for my shot. I stay leaned over as I take in his movements. When he begins to walk toward me, I stand fully and contemplate my next move. I'm not talking about my next move on the table, I'm referring to the real game we're playing.

Two can play this game.

He walks behind me, making sure the tip of his dick and his fingers brush across my lower back, then over my ass cheeks. His breath against my ear hits before his words do. "You missed. Such a shame. I had something in mind for those beautiful tits. I can't leave *them* out." My nipples harden with his deep voice and the anticipation it promises.

I swallow and barely find my way through a solid sentence. "I'm sure you'll get your opportunity." God. I sound pathetic. I may as well whimper and melt with his every touch, because that's practically what's happening. He's so intense I can feel him pulling at me without our bodies even touching. Let alone what he does to me when we do touch.

He leans over the table and I finally notice the markings on his back. They accentuate the width across his shoulders, the narrow section of his lower back, and then expand over each of his ass cheeks. I can't help but appreciate the art in front of me as he moves to make his shot.

"Looks like it's my turn to be tortured." He stands and my eyes are drawn to his glow in the dark dick and palms as he moves toward me. I let him approach me and even stop breathing when he stops right in front of me.

His cock is practically reaching out for me and I set the urge to climb him and take a ride aside for now. I spread my fingers across his chest as I walk behind him. Allowing my nipples to brush over his back, I reach around and take his dick in my hand and slowly begin stroking him.

I make sure my tits move as I do. His internal moan settles deep within me as I make sure to move fast enough to bring him very close to his release. I stop mid stroke and press my palm against his thigh, slowly moving it around his ass before sliding back around to face him.

The tip of his cock touches my stomach and I feel a coolness from the moisture he leaves behind.

"Fuckkkk. I'm going to enjoy fucking with your mind sweetheart." He leans over the table again, this time missing his shot.

"Your turn." He stands quickly and I decide it's time to win this game. I need to feel what this man can do to me when he's given the go ahead. The intensity is killing me and I swear the lump in my throat is going to strangle me each time I get near him.

I take my time and make the shot, even though he's standing behind me swirling the ice around in his glass. His hands are instantly on my hips and his cock is setting between my ass cheeks before I even have the chance to stand up. The sound of him taking a drink fills the room just before I feel the coolness of ice on my lower back. "I'd love to watch you with the lights on." He's moving against me as he continues to talk.

"I want to see if your face will tell me as much as your body does." His hands move over me after the ice melts quickly on my heated skin. "Such a canvas. Tell me how long it's been since you've had a man touch you like I do." I refuse to answer him and push up, lifting my body from the table.

I stand in front of him, allowing my breaths to hit his chest while he continues to slide ice over my chest.

"A body like this should be cherished." He slides the ice over my right nipple before he takes it into his mouth. His tongue is perfection as he pulls me closer until he has full access to my tits with his mouth and his hands full of my ass.

His tongue leaves a wet trail as he moves to my other nipple. "Before I'm done with you, this paint will look completely different." He moves his hands over my body, smearing all the paint in every direction. I look down and notice the glowing swirls creating an entirely different look.

My entire body is on fire waiting for him to touch me in the perfect place. If he so much as brushes across my clit right now, I'm positive I'll orgasm.

He stands fully, moving my chin up until my lips meet his. He brushes across mine just before he speaks. "Your turn again." Then he slowly runs his tongue over my puckered lips before he steps back, leaving me begging for more.

The game goes on for another half hour with us slowly torturing each other to the brink of orgasm, until it's finally down to just the eight ball.

I seriously don't know how much longer I can hang on, without breaking down and just finishing myself off right here in front of him.

It's his turn and I know without a doubt, that he could've

gotten that last ball in about three different times by now. I think he *wants* me to win.

So I do.

Without saying a word, he lifts me back up onto the pool table for the third time of the night and drops to his knees in front of me.

His mouth crashes against my pussy, his tongue devouring me as if he's been waiting all night to do this again.

"Fuck! You're so wet."

I'm so on edge that there's no way this is going to last more than two minutes.

He growls against my pussy, before sucking my clit into his mouth and roughly sucking it, while slipping two of his thick fingers into my pussy and sliding them in and out.

With the combination of his mouth, tongue and fingers, I lose it, coming harder than I've came in years.

Scratch that . . . probably harder than I've came in my entire life.

He stills his fingers, but gently runs his tongue over my pussy as if wanting every last drop of my arousal, knowing that he's the one who caused me to completely come undone.

I hadn't even realized my thighs were squeezing the life out of his head, until now. Now that I'm sitting here breathing as if I've just run a marathon.

Relaxing, I release his head and allow myself to take a few deep breaths and slowly release them.

The whole room spins around me as I stare up at the ceiling trying to make out the shadows and roughly grip my hair.

That's when a knock sounds at the door, bringing me down from my high and making me jump to reach for my clothing once again. I'm reaching frantically when the sound of the door knob turning throws me into a slight panic.

"One fucking minute," Lynx growls out.

Releasing an irritated breath, he reaches for his jeans and slips them on. I can only imagine that he's trying hard to adjust his large erection so he can cover it up.

"Thanks for the game," I stammer. "It's definitely time to go this time." I'm so out of breath, that I struggle to even get the words out.

I don't wait for him to speak, I just unlock the door and jump back when I almost run right into a tall figure with a glowing cowboy hat.

"Pardon me, Darlin'," he says in a sexy as sin Southern accent. Then he looks around me. "Didn't mean to interrupt, Boss."

"You didn't," I say quickly. "I was just leaving."

"Wait."

I ignore Lynx's demand and take off down the hall and down the stairs, getting lost in the crowd.

It takes me a few minutes, but I finally find the person who took my things on the way in and desperately reach for my phone to call Remi.

She answers on the second ring.

"Come and get me. Please hurry."

"Are you okay?" She sounds wide awake as if she's been waiting on me.

"I'm fine. I'm just tired," I breathe into the phone, while finding a quiet spot on the lawn. "Can you leave right now?"

"Yeah." I hear her keys shaking in the background. "On my way. Meet me where I dropped you off."

"Thank you, Remi."

I hang up and begin pacing as I shove my phone back into my purse.

"Holy shit," I say to myself. "This was not supposed to

happen. He's your boss . . . and the most desired man on the Internet."

Shit. Shit. Fuck . . .

Chapter TEN

Lynx

"WHAT THE ACTUAL FUCK!" I roll over and rub a hand over my face when I'm woken up by a sloppy tongue licking across the length of my face.

I growl under my breath when I realize who or rather *what* the tongue belongs to. There's a bulldog puppy in my fucking bed, panting down at me from above my face.

"Fucking Blaze," I mumble under my breath, while sitting up and grabbing for the dog's tag. "Alpha. That fucker would name you after my damn mansion."

Still tired as shit, I rub the dog's head and jump to my feet to throw some underwear on so I can find Blaze and rip the fucker a new asshole.

No one else would be dumb enough to bring in a dog without talking to me first. He has a lot of fucking explaining to do. Especially now that my sheets are covered in puppy drool and dog hair. Alpha is right under my feet the entire time I make my way through the house.

I search through the top floor, looking like a damn maniac, while calling out Blaze's name. He's not in his room or anywhere up here.

When I make it down to the kitchen, Knox, Levi and Rome are moping around, suffering from a major hangover.

"Where's Blaze? And why is there a fucking dog here?"

Knox shrugs. "Haven't seen him since last night."

"I don't know. Same here." Rome is one of the seven guys living here in the house. He's been with Alphachat.com for a few months and is really pulling in a decent amount of calls a week. The kid really has potential.

At twenty-one; he's the youngest Alpha in the house. Knox being the oldest at twenty-seven.

"When you see that dick, tell him to find me."

Levi just mumbles something, not making any damn sense at all.

I walk over to the fridge for a water. Alpha follows my every move, looking up at me as I slam my water back, drinking every last drop.

"You thirsty?" I lift a brow and look around for a dish that I can throw some water in. "Here you go, Bud. Enjoy."

I walk away, expecting him to stay and drink, but the little shit just continues to follow me.

"There's water and food upstairs." Knox stands up straight. "His heavy drinking woke me up this morning. I had to go and see what it was. Blaze's drunk ass was mumbling over the phone late last night about how he wanted a puppy, but I didn't think he'd actually end up with one."

"Of course he would end up with one. I wonder which one of his clients couldn't wait to show up here with a puppy." I know how these females work, that's why I have to watch what I say. They look for any and every reason to come see me.

Some of them I don't ever want to see again, then there's Rebel.

"If you see his ass . . . Tell him I'm looking for him." I leave them to their headaches and the damn mess scattered in every direction. At least my room wasn't included in the disaster aftermath of the party.

I check my emails hoping she would've sent something through the Alphachat.com website, but she didn't. Disappointment washes over me again just like it did when she rushed from the house last night.

I could see her on the lawn waiting for her ride, but chose not to approach her. The moonlight allowed me to watch her in a panic and I knew going to her would only make it worse.

Thoughts of her tortured me all night and it was hell trying to go to bed with that fucking hard on she caused. I should've fucked just any random in the house, but I didn't feel like playing the game to get them out of my bed afterwards.

Rebel has gotten to me. Her every fucking move intrigued me last night and honestly I wouldn't have been able to fuck anyone else in the pitch black without thinking about her the entire time.

My hand had to do the job just so I could fucking go to sleep.

I sit in the chair and stare at the monitor, trying to decide how to deal with this Rebel situation. I could call her into the club for some ridiculous made-up meeting and see how she responds to me, or I could send her a message on the chat page.

Fuck it. I decide to do both and see which one she responds to first.

I start typing as the phone begins to ring.

"Mornin', Boss. What can I do for you so damn early?" Brit answers and I cringe thinking about how I'm going to get Rebel's phone number without being obvious.

"Morning. I need you to get all of my new bartenders called in for a mandatory meeting today at two. I'll be training on the specialty drinks and if they can't make it to that meeting, tell them not to bother coming to work again."

"Damn. I'm on it. I think you have three new ones other than the guys. Do you want your guys to sit in on it too?"

"No. They know their shit. I'll be in a few minutes before two, so gather anything you want me to sign before I get there."

"I'm on it." I hit end on the call before she can say anything else. Typing the last few words, I reread it just to make sure it's what I want to say.

> *You ran out on me just before it got real good. Next time it'll be my dick causing you to whimper.*

That pretty much says what I want to say. She won't get the opportunity to run the next time I get my hands on her.

I take a very long hot shower and do as much business admin work as I can stand before I decide it's time to hit the gym and work out some of this aggression.

The way she looked last night under my hands has been fucking with me. I wish like fuck I would've just turned on the lights and did things the right way. Now I'm left with part of it all being my imagination.

She was into all the games and I have to say that turns me on more than anything about her. I love a woman who isn't afraid to keep me guessing in the bedroom. It makes for one hell of an adventure.

Too many times I've been in the monotonous relationship where everything is the same over and over. I can't fucking stand that shit. And I can't stand being the only one to have any creativity when it comes to that stuff.

Damn it. My dick is twitching again thinking about her as I work the last set of the curls I intend to do. I catch my hard on in the mirror of the gym and notice I'm not the only one who sees it. The blonde that I've fucked at least four times after a gym session is watching me from the bench she's pretending to still be working on.

Not wanting to deal with her today, I grab a towel and start walking for the front door. I know if I walk to the lockers, she'll be right on my ass. Hell, I'm pretty sure some of the guys think she should just have a locker in there herself for as much time as she spends in there.

"Lynx." I hear her behind me just as I get to my truck.

"Not today. I'm late." I close the door and start the engine, pulling away before she has the time to even consider opening the door.

Fuck. Rebel. I will be taking this shit out on you when I get my hands on you again.

Now I find myself sweaty as hell and not enough time to go home and shower again unless I break my own two o'clock time demand. I look down once more at my soaked shirt and choose to go home and take that shower.

Calling Brit one last time to delay the newbies long enough for me, I speed home and pull up to a giant delivery truck parked in the driveway.

Stepping around to see what's being delivered, I instantly smile at what I see. "Alright, Boss man, where does this go?" Nash is looking at me surprised as I start to examine the cross.

"In my room." I start to think of all the ways I'll have fun with this new toy while I pleasure torture someone specific in my mind.

"I figured that was Blaze's." Nash's voice comes from behind me now while I take in all the hooks and the wood grain of this beast.

"It might be. I'll order whoever another one. Today. This one is mine."

"I'm gonna love living in this house." I can hear him talking as he walks away.

I run my fingers over the Saint Andrew's cross and tell the delivery guys to follow me. I'll have to order another one of these soon to pay back whoever originally ordered this, but right now, this one is mine and I'd pay top dollar to someone to make sure of it.

Stepping into my room, I direct them to the section against the west wall that is never on camera.

I had the extra area in my room built so I could have a small living area to escape if needed. After seeing this cross, I think I'll be using this side of the room for a few other items instead.

I hand the delivery guys a couple hundred dollar bills as a tip and quickly get into the shower. The excitement I feel about seeing Rebel is very new to me. I'm not used to wanting a woman this much.

Glancing at the clock as I get in, I see that it's already after two so I make it a very quick one. The anticipation of seeing her has me a little more excited than I'll ever admit to anyone.

I'm curious about how she'll act with me today.

I pull into my parking spot at the back of the club and slip in the back door as usual. This door opens up to the main hallway that goes by my office in the back. I can hear Brit talking to someone, so I move toward her and make eye contact with Rebel just as I round the corner.

Fuck. She's sexy as fuck and my dick notices instantly. Her eyes move back to Brit almost instantly as she rambles on about some bullshit I can't even hear her saying.

There's one other guy standing beside her and I wish now that I would've told them all to come in separately.

"Alright, sorry I'm late. Let me show you both around the bar a little. I want nothing but perfection in the hands of my patrons so today you'll learn what I expect from my bartenders." I walk past them and open the main door to the bar, allowing each of them to pass through while I hold it open.

She doesn't look at me when she walks by and I fight the urge to stop her by gripping her long sexy hair in my hands and pulling her back against my chest. Instead, I watch her ass in those shorts as she walks in front of me.

Fuck my life. I want that ass.

Chapter ELEVEN

Rebel

I CAN FEEL HIM STARING into me the second he walks up. There's no doubt he recognized me last night. I know that for sure now.

I'm not even sure why I hoped he hadn't. The intensity he carries weighs so heavy on me as we stand here and listen to Brit walk us through the things I already know.

He's standing behind me and it feels awkward trying to act normal after what we did last night. I'm just glad the bar is closed right now and I'm only having to fool Brit and this new guy beside me.

"Have them start by making the specialty martinis today, then we can work on some of the others a different day." Lynx's deep voice goes through me the second he begins to talk.

He sits at the bar while Brit moves us around the back side to set us each up a different area to work. She hands me the drink card and I go to work. This is all second nature to me and before the poor other guy has a chance to find the right bottles I'm handing the glass to Brit.

She reaches across the bar and gives it to Lynx, who watches me the entire time he takes a drink. I feel like I'm standing in front of an audience as I wait for his response.

"Perfect." I almost don't hear him as he exhales through his response. His eyes catch mine and I can't help but look away just as they do.

The things this man can do to me without even touching my body confuse me.

Brit hands me the next two cards, so I start making both of those. These drinks aren't anything I haven't made before, just premium bottles of alcohol which I've always preferred anyway.

I hand her both of these glasses and wait for his response to both.

"That one is too sweet for my taste, but it always is." He sets the chocolate martini back on the bar and reaches for the other. He nods his approval and moves to try the first one the other guy has managed to make.

This goes on for about eight martinis and it eventually gets easier to move around him.

"Brit, you finish with him and I'm going to work on some paperwork with her in my office. She never had the chance to finish up hers that first night she started." My heart sinks knowing I'm about to be alone with him, but I follow him to his office anyway.

The way he moves reminds me of last night in so many ways and it's so hard not to be turned on right now, even though I know I should be far from it.

He opens the door allowing me to enter, just before he closes it and adjusts the lock. My nerves begin to fuck with me even more as I stand waiting for him to speak.

His fierce stare almost intimidates me, but I remember how intense he was last night. This is Lynx Kade and if I was to bet, I'd guess this man is always this serious.

"Are you still aching to feel me inside you?" His words hit me just before his hand touches my back. Just before he pulls me against his chest and just before I feel his cock bulging through his jeans as it rests against my hip.

"Yes." My body is already betraying me, so why not let my mouth.

"Then why did you run?" He releases his hold on my back to move my hair from my face.

"I had to before it went there."

"Why?"

"You're my boss."

"Fine. You're fired." He steps away from me as we continue to talk and uses his hand to guide me to sit in the chair across from his desk.

"You can't fire me. I need this job." I sit with perfect posture as I try to work through the chaos of emotions he causes.

"I have a different job for you. I need an assistant." He sits back in his chair and allows his eyes to rake over my chest a few times.

"You'd still be my boss," I point out.

"True." He continues to watch me in silence for a while before he leans forward and begins to move a few papers on the desk. I watch his dark hair and even catch myself licking my bottom lip as I look at his.

"I make the rules when it comes to my companies. I don't ever fuck an employee. It just gets too messy, so I agree." I listen to him continue and even contemplate quitting when I see his arm muscles flex when he sits back once more. "So if you'd like to make even more money than you do here, I need an assistant at the house."

"What exactly do you need an assistant for?" I ask hesitantly. He smiles as he watches over me.

"Paperwork, billing, scheduling, updating the webpage with all the new pricing and anything else that comes up as the company grows."

I think about what he's saying. It would be a step up from working in the bar late at night making drinks. "I can do that."

He stands instantly and grabs his keys.

"Great. You can start tomorrow. Be there at nine and I'll show you around. I assume you remember where the house is."

I follow him to the door and notice the coldness between us. "Yes I do, thank you."

"Don't thank me yet. You have no idea what you're in for." I nod, knowing my world is about to change immensely.

"See you tomorrow, Rebel." He closes the door as I step into the hall. I don't even have a chance to respond to him.

A house full of men with me there every day. *What could possibly go wrong?*

"ARE YOU DAMN KIDDING ME? You get to work with them all every day. Tell me again how you didn't fuck Lynx and I'll continue to not believe you." Remi freaks and scares me as her voice blasts through the speakers in my Jeep.

"I didn't. We came really close, but we did not fuck."

"Yet. You forgot the rest of that sentence. You didn't fuck yet. But it's coming."

I swear this woman drives me crazy sometimes.

"He's my boss and you know how I need this job. I can't mess up this kind of money."

"Well, I think fucking your boss is hot. When the hell did I start living vicariously through you, because damn it my life is lame as fuck lately. I need you to work me in to that little circle of yours."

"He said I'd make more than I would at the club, so I know he'll pay very well. This is where we're different, Remi. You would fuck him and mess up the job. I won't do that."

"Riiiiight. I saw the fucked-up smeared paint all over you last night. I'd say you'd do more than you pretend. Remember, I know you better than you know yourself." She's right and damn it, I'm not the least bit sorry about last night. It just may torture me forever while I work in that house, but it's something I'll have to deal with.

"I'll see you tonight. I'm making lasagna so make sure you don't miss our date." I remind her of our plans. She's the one that reserved tonight for us to hang out. It was supposed to be my last night off for a few days so she wanted to spend time together.

"I'll be there in a few hours. I have some errands to run and then you're mine for the evening. See you soon." She hangs up just as I pull into the driveway. I want to take a nap before she forces me to stay up late on a Game of Thrones binge.

Stepping into my room I instantly think about Lynx on the computer, which has me turning it on for some damn reason that I can't explain.

Looking closer, I see that he's messaged me. It instantly gets my heart racing.

> *You ran out on me just before it got real good. Next time it'll be my dick causing you to whimper.*

Oh my god. How am I supposed to work with this man? I look at the time stamp on the message and see that it's from before our meeting. I'm just going to assume he's now changed his take on what he plans to do with me. After all, he also expressed how bad of an idea it would be to mix business with pleasure.

I'm scrolling through a few of his pictures that must've just got added recently, just as another message from him pops up.

I see you looking at my pictures.

Shit. My heart sinks and I panic just as I realize he can't see anything. I disconnected the video feed on my laptop after the last disaster. Responding quickly, I decide to try to end this mess with him.

No you don't.

He's typing instantly and I wait impatiently for his reply to pop up while my heart begins to race faster.

You've read my message and it still shows you're logged in . . . so what else would you be doing? Unless you're pleasuring yourself again.

Holy shit. He's sending heat straight through me and I don't know whether to be embarrassed or turned on with his straight forwardness.

I'm not responding to that.

You don't have to. I'll see you tomorrow morning, unless you'd like to see more of me tonight . . .

We've already established the rules.

Fuck the rules. Rules are meant to be broken.

And with that, I close my laptop knowing I'll be putting myself in complete torture working with him. He will make me crazy and if he so much as breathes on me, I'm liable to climb him and fuck him myself. I won't even have to worry about him trying to get to me. I'm more worried about me going for him at this point.

I can tell he likes to play games. It'll be interesting seeing how he deals with me tomorrow morning.

That nap I need won't come easy now that he has me all worked up. I lay down and think about last night. He made me feel so special. I've never been treated like he handled me last night and I have to say I loved it.

I have two options.

One . . . work for him as long as I can while fucking him. It's just a matter of time before something blows up and that will be a disaster. I could always find a different job at that point.

Or two . . . keep my distance from him in that department and make the job last even longer. Get a cushion for myself so I can really work on my own business before I walk away from the job with Lynx for either reason.

This just won't be a long term job for me in either scenario, so this is tough. I think we'll need to lay out some ground rules before I take on this job with him.

The problem is . . . I'm not so sure he'll allow that.

Number One . . . Don't speak because your voice makes me crazy.

Shit, this isn't going to work.

Chapter Twelve

Lynx

I'M STILL TRYING TO GET my papers organized when I hear the doorbell ring. It was another late night taking calls, with Rebel flashing through my damn mind. I've wanted to kick my own ass a few times knowing how I am when something is off limits or out of reach.

The way she keeps slipping out of my fucking fingers is making me damn cranky, but I plan to make sure that's rectified soon. I only agreed with her at the office to get her to my house. She can pretend to be all high and mighty with her rules, but she can't forget how I've had her sprawled open and naked in multiple rooms of my house already.

Fuck. Her tits are completely covered today. She's going to play hard to get. That's ok though, I already know she's going to be worth the wait.

"Mornin', Rebel. Did you dream about me last night?"

"Good morning." She doesn't respond to my question, trying hard to look as unaffected as possible. "We need to talk before I agree to work for you."

"Alright. Would you like to see my office in the daylight . . . or how about my game room? If those don't work, I can take you to my bedroom where most of my work is actually done." She hesitates before she answers.

"Your office will work." She starts to walk up the stairs and I follow behind. I want to grab her ass and lay her right her on the steps to show her who I am, but I don't.

She sits at my desk like this office is hers, leaving me the choice to either sit across from her in the guest chair or in the chaise lounge that she sucked me off on last night.

I choose the chaise, of course allowing my arms to support my head while I lay back and watch the memories flash through her mind.

She stands quickly and begins to walk around the room as she talks.

"We need boundaries. Can you handle that if I come to work for you here? I really need a job, so I can't do anything to mess it up."

"I'll give you a year contract." I decide to make this easy on her.

"What if I hate working for you in a week?"

"Then you can work at the club for that long and you won't have to deal with me." She leans against the side of my desk as she takes me in. I love letting her watch me and I'm wondering in the back of my mind what she'd do if I unzipped my pants and started stroking my cock in front of her.

"I don't want special treatment."

"You sure about that? Because I'm thinking you'll change your mind." I stand and face her, but she won't look at me as I walk up to her. Lifting her face to meet mine, I try one last time to get her to bite.

"I'm real good at special treatment. Some would say I'm the best." She swallows as she watches my lips. I can see her struggle and this makes me happy. She needs to want me to touch her as bad as I've been wanting to fuck her.

Taking this signal as my win, I move to sit in the chair behind my desk.

"Can we talk about my exact job specifications?"

"Yes. You work Monday through Friday, nine to two. I'll have work for you each day and if you finish early, I'll let you go home. Or . . . I guess you could stay longer if you'd like. I need you to start with scheduling. I'm filling up four weeks out now, but if anyone cancels we move someone into the open time slot. An hour wasted is a lot of fucking money and I don't like losing easy money."

"I can do that." She sits across from me as we continue talking business and fights to look conformable, but I can tell she's still worked up and on edge.

"I have regulars. They pay good money to be on a weekly rotation. You don't ever fill their time slots with anyone else. Also, I need you to bill everyone a day in advance. If they don't pay by the morning of, they get canceled. No exceptions. In fact, that's how you got your slot." I purposely mention her watching me on camera. She squirms in her chair while I watch her closely.

"What the fuck happened during your call anyway?"

"What do you mean?" Her face turns slightly pink.

"The camera was black, then all of a sudden the room was spinning. Tell me you like it rough and humped the computer right off the table while you watched me."

"No. I spilled my coffee while I tried to stay awake." Her quick response and red face tells me she's lying. I know she is, because she actually came to my party.

"Well then, it won't be anything for you to work in this house then. I have six of us living here with two more guys that could come and go. At any moment they may decide to have a show in the kitchen or a bathroom. Hell, maybe even in the living room. So don't be surprised if you see someone stroking their cock out of nowhere." Her eyes go wide and I love that I can shock her.

"Can you ask them to keep me out of the videos?"

"Yes. I'll tell them all to keep you out of it." In fact, I'll threaten them all to stay the fuck away from her. "Anything else?" I have to ask her for any further requests, but I have a feeling she'll be adding to this list as we go. I plan to test her in every way possible.

"I can't think of anything right now. When would you like me to start?"

"How about right now?" I'm not ready to be done with her today. She needs to be way more bothered before she leaves my house. I want her thinking about me all night long.

"Sounds good."

"Alright. First, I need you to take a few pictures of me out by the pool. My page is outdated with old photos that I stuck back up and it always helps the business when I update the inventory shots." Making my way to the door, I let her follow me through the house. "The guys will all need new shots soon, so don't post any that are real similar to mine on the webpage once they get some sent in. I like to keep it original where my shots are concerned."

"I can do that." Her breath hitches and her voice cracks as I drop my pants and hand her the camera from the table. I planned this little shoot this morning, knowing I'd need to get her out here.

My naked ass is all she sees as I walk away, tossing my shirt into her chest. I stand next to the waterfall and let the water cover my dick, my ass is showing from the side as she slowly makes her way across the pool to get a better angle.

She's watching me closely with each step and I can tell she's saying something to herself.

"What? I can't hear you?" I say it on purpose to let her know I can see her talking. She's not used to someone like me and it's going to be a blast pulling her out of her comfort zone on a damn daily basis.

"I said you're crazy." She aims the camera lens at me and I work my sex appeal directly at her. This isn't for the webpage, it's for her.

Holding my dick in my hand, I stroke it allowing the water to fall all around me. She's kneeling and zoomed in, so I can only imagine what she's seeing.

I turn and give her the full view and she looks over the top of the camera at me before she's looking through the lens again. Moving it side to side, I give her plenty to remember me by. The length of my dick is something I'm very fucking proud of and known for. She's seen it, but right now she's seeing it up close, zoomed in so far I'm guessing she can see the bulging veins throbbing against my palms.

I'll be sure to send her these pictures once she leaves.

With my palm held out, I give it a few loud smacks from my dick. It's a signature move and something I get requested to do often.

She stops taking pictures to look at me again.

"Is the camera broke?" I yell at her from across the water and watch her stand fully. She's turned on. I can see it in her flushed face.

"No. I think I got all of these, maybe you should do some in the water."

"Good idea. Why don't you stand over me and get the blurred image of my dick under the water?" She nods slowly and I can tell she was hoping I'd get under water and quit showing her my dick. She has to remember that I'm used to this. This is what I do for a living.

I dive into the pool and go for the fully dripping wet look. Propping my elbows on the side of the pool right beneath her, I raise my body up just below the water level and give her the best view I can.

Looking back, I can see that she's not even remotely close enough to capture the shot I'd love her to get.

"Come closer. Go over my shoulder and aim down my chest and stomach." I can hear her kneeling behind me and my dick gets harder knowing she's this near. I'm glad I went for the heated pool.

She's near my ear and I want to drag her in this pool and fuck her. I listen to the sound of the camera clicking picture after picture. Moving my hand over my cock, I do a few teasing strokes and she slows the clicking to almost none.

"It would be better if it was your hand stroking me." My voice is just loud enough for her to hear. She stands and instantly starts to walk away.

"I can't work for you."

Perfect. Now we can fuck.

Chapter Thirteen

Rebel

I STILL CAN'T BELIEVE THE nerve of him this morning. I've been home for three hours. Three damn hours and he's still all that I can think about.

He's taking my rules of working for him as a joke and pushing me, because he knows damn well that he's the only one that makes rules when it comes to him.

Photo shoot my ass. Lynx probably won't use even one of those pictures to update his profile. He was just trying to get a rise out of me and it worked.

I'm doing my best to make sure that I can keep this job and all he wants to do is give me every reminder that he can that I want nothing more than to sleep with my boss.

I'm really close to actually not going back tomorrow. I keep telling myself that over and over, but there's a part of me that wants to say fuck it and push him back.

I'm no fucking pushover. I have fight in me and I'll show it if I have to.

With my mind going all over the place, I find myself sitting in front of my computer and logging onto the website.

If I'm going to be working on Alphachat.com and keeping things updated, then I might as well get a closer look at what I'll be jumping into.

I spend the next hour checking out every last detail that I can. I'm so zoned in that I practically jump out of my chair when my computer dings with a message from Lynx.

Waiting for those pictures that I promised you?

No. If you must know . . . I'm studying.

Studying. You'll have plenty to study later, even though I have a feeling the only thing you truly want to be studying right now is my cock.

Just then one of the pictures that I took from earlier pops up, causing me to gasp and my whole body to heat up with the same need that I felt earlier while taking his pics.

I don't know why this even surprises me in the slightest. He's Lynx Kade and this man truly has no filter or nothing to be ashamed of. Especially that beautiful dick of his and he knows it.

The shot he decided to send me is one from the pool from when I was looking down at him. The water is so clear that it gives me a perfect view of his very hard dick, standing at full attention.

And for some reason . . . I'm staring at it so hard that my vision begins to blur.

You can stop staring now.

I'm not. And my boss sending me naked pictures is very unprofessional. If you must know.

Even when you're the one to take them, BadGirl@heart? Better get used to it if you plan on working at the Alpha House, because you're going to be staring at that website a hell of a lot of hours of the day. Seeing me naked is part of the job. You need to learn to handle it.

Shit! He's completely right.

Then maybe I don't want the job.

You do.

What makes you so sure?

The fact that you've been on my site for the last hour. Here's another pic. Edit it and I'll add it to today's pay.

Are you serious? Did you miss the part where I said I couldn't work for you?

No. Heard it loud and clear. See you tomorrow at nine.

He doesn't give me a chance to respond, before he disconnects our chat, leaving me with a heated face.

With frustration, I slam my laptop closed and yell.

"Whoa, killer. What did that poor laptop ever do to you?" Remi throws her purse on the kitchen counter, before plopping down on the couch and looking over at me.

"I'm completely frustrated with my new job right now, Remi. I don't know if I can handle it."

"You can. For all of us other women, you better figure it out." She smiles really big and leans over the couch to show me that she's ready to listen. "So tell me about this *horrible* day that you had at the house that *every* woman is dying to get into. I'm all ears."

"Where do I even start? Oh yeah." I stand up and start pacing, completely heated when I begin to play the morning over in my head. "He totally ignored my ground rules for working for him as if it was all just a joke to him. Then he had me take nude photos of him, while I had to practically watch him stroke his dick in front of me. How am I supposed to work like this? He's my boss. Then he said it would be better if I was the one stroking his dick for him. What kind of boss says that?"

"Oh, God. A hot one, Rebel. That's who. What the fuck!" She jumps up from the couch and rushes to the fridge. She pulls out a bottle of wine. "Come in here and sit. Stop that pacing shit."

Taking a deep breath, I take a seat on one of the stools and grab the glass of wine that she pours for me.

"Very good," she says as I tilt it back. "Your ass needs to calm down for a second. I haven't seen you this worked up in a long time, Babe."

"I don't know why I'm letting him get to me so much." I take another sip and then slowly and calmly release a breath.

"I know why." Her smile broadens. "Because you want to fuck him."

"Thanks for pointing out the obvious," I huff. "That makes it a huge problem. If I didn't want to, then I'd be able to do this job with no problem. His dirty mouth wouldn't bother me and taking pics of him holding his dick wouldn't corrupt my mind all day and make it hard to function."

"So what did you tell him?"

"I told him that I couldn't work for him and I walked away."

I stand up and take my wine glass with me.

"Are you fucking serious?" She runs up to me and grabs my wine glass away, right as I'm about to press it to my lips. "You can't just quit. I'd die to have your job, Woman. You're going back tomorrow even if I have to wake you up and drag you there myself."

"You just want to sneak into the Alpha Mansion," I point out. "Maybe I should work him up by letting you go in my place. See how he likes it when someone doesn't follow *his* rules."

Remi lifts a brow, seriously looking as if she's considering talking me into that idea. "I wouldn't argue with you on that, but then you'd probably get fired anyway. As much as I'm dying inside to step foot into that house, I don't want you messing up this opportunity. It's good money. Forget everything else for two seconds and think about that. Forget about the fact that your boss is drop dead gorgeous and wants to get into your pants."

She does have a point. I'd probably never make that kind of money anywhere else.

"And the fact that you get to spend time with the other Alpha boys." She grabs a magazine and starts fanning herself off. "They spend most of their time naked. I hate you."

She tosses the magazine down and walks away.

"I love you too, Remi!" I scream after her.

"If you do, then you'll go back to that damn house tomorrow and work and secretly send me pics of the guys naked. Just remember that . . ."

"Funny, Remi."

She pokes her head out from her bedroom doorway. "Not trying to be. I'm going to take a nap before my shift at the diner. You just drink that wine of yours and think about all of the reasons that you *shouldn't* quit."

I shake my head and laugh to myself when she closes herself inside her room and then opens it real fast to yell at me. "Got it!"

"Got it. Jeez, Remi."

After Remi left for the diner two hours ago, I needed to get out of the house for a bit, so I took a long run and then went to the grocery store.

It's well past ten now and my mind is still stuck on Lynx and this damn job that I *really* want, but am trying hard to convince myself that I don't.

I'm not going to lie . . . my body wants to march back to that mansion right now and let Lynx do anything and everything he wants to me, but my head keeps telling me that I need to be strong.

If this boss, employee relationship is going to work, then it needs to be just that. Plain and simple.

I go to work.

He tells me what needs to be done.

I do my job.

I leave.

Simple. Right?

I know it's going to be anything but simple, yet I think I'm up for the challenge.

Sitting in my bed with my laptop in my lap, I begin surfing the web, while popping grapes in my mouth.

After about ten minutes, I get bored and find myself staring at Alphachat.com again. I decide to pull up that second picture that he asked me to edit.

There's *nothing* to edit. Is he insane? It's beautiful and he knows it.

Him completely naked, holding his dick under a damn waterfall. What could possibly make this better than it already is?

It's working perfectly fine at getting me all hot and bothered and I have a feeling that he just wanted to give me a reason to stare at him naked.

Jerk.

Leaving the picture as is, I close out his message and find myself looking at Lynx's profile.

The thing I've learned about the website is that the boys can see when any of their clients are logged in, but we can't see them unless they want to be seen.

Very smart on their part.

I can't even imagine how many chat requests they'd receive otherwise.

Staring at the screen, I get frustrated with myself, realizing that I'm waiting for a message to pop up from Lynx.

"What the hell am I doing? This is fucking ridiculous."

I quickly shut down my computer and shove it aside, wanting to kick my own ass for even being slightly curious about what Lynx might be up to right now.

Each time I log into that site, I'm leaving myself open and vulnerable for him to work his way even further under my skin and cloud my thoughts.

He's my damn boss and I'm going to keep it that way as long as I can . . .

Chapter Fourteen

Lynx

SHIT. WHEN I SAW REBEL'S name pop up last night proving that she was online, I wanted nothing more than to cancel my call for the night and ask her why she was "studying" the chat site again.

Her being on so late gave me all the confirmation that I needed to know that she'll be here at my door in less than thirty minutes, ready to keep her job.

I just hope she's ready for everything this job entails. I'm not going to lie; my guys are a rough bunch to put up with. Half of the fuckers run around with their dicks swinging when they're in a rush to prepare for more than one show and want to grab a quick bite in between or a prop that they left in a different room.

Hell . . . it took my ass time to get used to it and I'm one of those fuckers running around sometimes.

The pawing at my door starts up again, causing me to stand up and open my office door. Alpha has been sitting outside my damn door since I closed myself in here more than thirty minutes ago.

Very fucking conveniently, Blaze has found every excuse

to be too busy to talk ever since I found Alpha in my bed a few mornings ago.

"Blaze. In my office. We need to talk."

I sit down in my chair and Alpha instantly lays down at my feet.

Blaze pokes his head in my office a few minutes later, looking like his ass has just rolled out of bed. The fucker definitely had a rough night. "Yeah. What's up?" He promptly looks down at Alpha by my feet, before looking back up at me. "Isn't the fucker cute?"

I run my hand over my face in frustration. "You know the rules. Maybe next time you can include the whole fucking house in your decision to bring an animal inside these doors."

"Sorry, my man. It was a spur of the moment decision." He slaps his leg and calls Alpha to him. Alpha is quick to run across the carpet face planting into his leg, before falling over as Blaze begins to rub him with both hands.

"You mean a drunken decision," I retort. "You're lucky mini fucking Alpha there has grown on me a bit and that the other guys have been good with helping clean up after him."

Blaze flashes a smile and picks Alpha up, talking in his face. "I was counting on you being a cute little shit. Welcome to the Alpha House, Little Guy."

He walks away with a smile on his face while he continues to talk to the dog and I shake my head at that guy.

He's actually done better than I thought he would. I knew he'd be a mess, but what he brings to the business far out-weighs any shit I've had to deal with so far. As long as he continues to be a great profit, he can do whatever the fuck he wants.

After Blaze disappears, I look over at the clock to see that it's just five minutes 'til nine. Just then we get a buzz at the gate that brings a smile to my face. I know it's Rebel. She can't stay away and I love knowing I have that kind of power over her.

One of the other guys must let her in, because I don't even get a chance to, before the gates are opening for her and I look on the screen to see her driving her black Jeep inside.

I gather the last of the paperwork up and try to decide how to make today an eventful work day for me with Rebel right by my side.

When I walk out of my office to let her in the front door, I look down to see Rome already standing by the opened door, shirtless and in his boxer briefs.

"Damn, what a great wake up call." He looks Rebel over as she steps inside, her eyes wandering over Rome's ripped body.

My blood instantly boils as he reaches out and grips her waist.

"Hands off," I growl over the railing. "She's here to work, not *fuck* any of you dicks."

Rebel looks up at me with a slight smirk, as if me being bothered by Rome touching her makes her happy.

She turns back to Rome. "Thanks for letting me in."

Rome lets out a small moan, while looking her over, but drops his hand from her, immediately. He knows if he doesn't then he'll lose the fucker.

"Not a problem." He nods toward the kitchen and presses down on the front of his briefs. The fucker has a boner. "I'll be drowning myself in coffee. Have fun."

Rebel watches Rome walk away, before she walks up the stairs, storms past me and closes herself inside the office.

Well shit . . .

Now I really need to find a way to get her out of there and next to me.

SMIRKING, I WATCH AS REBEL moans and groans, while looking for what I told her I needed help finding.

She won't be finding it anywhere near there. Trust me. I just wanted a way to get her in my room.

"It's nowhere over here. I've looked three times. Are you sure it's . . ." With a look of frustration, she glances my way and freezes when she notices me taking my shirt off. "What the hell are you doing?"

"Taking a call."

"Don't you dare hit that . . ."

Before she can finish, I hit the accept button and *Racylady28*'s seductive voice comes through the black screen.

"There's the sexy man I've been dreaming about for the last twenty-eight days. Oh my . . . Lynx. Have you gotten even hotter since last month?"

I cock a brow and glance to Rebel's side of the room when she growls out her frustration of being trapped in my room.

Ignoring her question, I finish taking my shirt off and toss it over at Rebel, just to work her up even more. I love seeing her so uptight and sexually frustrated, because I'm going to be the one to release that frustration and bring the animal out in her.

She flashes me the middle finger when my shirt lands on her face and then falls to her hand. "Fucker," she mouths.

"Oh I like that," *Racylady28* purrs. "Your aggression is extremely sexy today. Now . . ." She pauses for a second. "I only have thirty minutes for break so let's work quickly before someone finds me hiding back here. Take your pants off and let me see you in those sexy briefs."

Biting my bottom lip, I pull the belt from the loops and then quickly strip out of my jeans, being sure to give Rebel a good view of my cock that is now hard from having her in the room, watching me.

She may be pretending that she's not into my live show, but the way she keeps wiping her palms down her jeans, tells me otherwise.

"Very nice. Now rub your dick through the fabric for me. Rub it nice and slow and show me how good it feels."

I feel Rebel's eyes on me as I take my hand and begin rubbing it over my hard length, while slowly running my tongue over my bottom lip.

"Oh. My. God. You are a beautiful creature, Lynx. I'd give my left tit to be able to take the place of your hand right now."

I give Rebel a cocky smirk, which only causes her to look even more pissed off than she did when I first hit that accept button, knowing damn well that she wanted to stay off camera.

The only way out of my room is on camera. I have her trapped and I can see it in her eyes that she wants to eat me alive right now.

"Lose the briefs and give me a good view of your nice firm ass. I want to memorize every single inch of your body by the time this call ends."

Following my client's demand, I pull my boxer briefs down, watching as Rebel's eyes widen when my erect cock springs free.

Watching her, I stroke it a few times, reminding her of our call last week.

"Hey," *Racylady28*'s voice cuts through, breaking up my show for Rebel. "I didn't ask you to touch it yet. Attention my way. Why do you keep looking over there?"

This gets Rebel to smile as if she's just thought of something.

I'm curious. Very fucking curious.

"Much better," *Racylady28* says when I turn back to face the camera. "Give me your full attention, while you slap that huge dick of yours against the palm of your hand. You know how much I love that."

I begin doing as she says, slapping my cock against my palm.

Out of my peripheral vision, I notice some movement from Rebel, but I fight hard to not pay attention. That is until I hear what sounds like the zipper of her jeans, slowly coming undone.

Oh fuck me!

I risk a quick glance her way, to see her shirt lifted above her bra as she's stepping out of her jeans, kicking them aside.

She flashes me a seductive smile, while slowly running her hand down her smooth stomach, letting it disappear into the top of her lacy thong.

"Over here, Lynx." I can hear the frustration in *Racylady28*'s voice, so I do my best to give her my full attention, when all I really want to do is slam Rebel against the wall and fuck her until she knows who's in control here.

"What next?" I growl out.

"Stroke it for me. Get it wet first with that oil you love so much."

Squirting some oil in my hand, my eyes connect with Rebel's and I can see the fire in them as she slowly begins sliding her hand around in her panties. I can tell she's putting her fingers inside her pussy by the way her fingers disappear and fuck me, I can't handle this shit.

She's torturing me and I'm sure she's getting me back for trapping her in here for my show.

She slides the lacy material to the side, giving me a full view of what she's doing.

I begin stroking my cock, while watching her finger herself. "Oh fuck," I moan.

"Lynx. . . . Lynx." *Racylady28* fights to get my attention, but it's stuck on Rebel looking so fucking beautiful as she slips her finger in and out of her wetness. I move closer to the screen so Racylady can't see me watching Rebel pleasure herself.

She lays against the wall and begins to move her other hand up her shirt. Her eyes are looking into mine and she continues to challenge me while I stroke myself in front of the camera.

Racylady's voice begins to annoy me because all I want to hear is Rebel. Her breath should be against my face or even against my cock and here I am fifteen fucking feet away.

"Fuck it!" I hit disconnect on the call and stalk toward Rebel with a purpose.

There's no way in hell I can take a call, while she's off to the side finger fucking herself and biting her damn lip like that.

She gives me a surprised look as I pick her up and slide her legs around my waist. Her eyes are dilated and I can tell she's turned on too.

"You want to play games?" I step away from the wall, taking her with me. "Then let's fuckin' play." I drop her on my bed and slide her panties off before I chase her up the mattress as she backs her way to the pillows. Her eyes never leave mine and I'm so fucking turned on right now that I can hardly stand the friction on my dick as it touches the blanket on the way to her.

I take her fingers and suck them into my mouth, tasting her wetness as I moan at the reminder of how she tastes.

"We shouldn't do this." Her words say one thing, but her body is telling me another.

"Too fucking late." I reach for a condom and watch her face while she watches my hands roll it on. The hungry look in her eyes matches mine and I'm literally aching to get inside this woman.

"Tell me you don't want my cock and I'll stop." I lean over and kiss her. "Tell me you don't want my lips all over your body." She begins to kiss me back and our tongues battle as we both fight for control. "Tell me you don't crave my tongue again and I'll stop."

I move down her body and quickly run my tongue over her and pull her clit into my mouth. She's squirming against the bed while I move my tongue in and out of her. "This pussy isn't for your fingers. It's for me. *My fingers, my tongue and my cock.*"

Her grip on the sheet tightens as I move my body over her completely. Normally I'd spend more time teasing her, but honestly we've already done that. We've literally been doing foreplay since we first laid eyes on each other so to say I'm ready is a fucking understatement.

I work her bra up over her tits and take in how gorgeous she really is. Seeing them in daylight makes it so much better. She closes her eyes when I begin to lick both nipples before I take each of them into my mouth and roughly suck them.

"Fucking gorgeous." I bite her nipple slightly and she grabs the back of my head, pulling me closer, with a slight moan.

"What are you doing to me?" Her words come out around the sexy sounds coming from her mouth, causing me to smile. I have her exactly where I want her. In my bed. Under me. Moaning against me.

I position myself over her and begin to slide into her, slowly, doing my best not to hurt her even though I'm dying to fuck her like I've never fucked before. "Fuck Rebel. You're tight as hell on my cock."

"Don't stop." She wraps her hands around my back as I thrust in harder each time, taking her deeper. She closes her eyes and leans her head back, releasing a moan mixed with pleasure and pain as I enter her again and again.

Fucking sexy. I never get tired of watching a woman take me in for the first time.

I start to move faster and harder with each thrust, while wrapping my hands into the back of her hair and pulling. "Fuck." She finally takes in *all* of me and opens her eyes to meet mine.

Towering over her, I fuck her while looking into her eyes every time she lets me.

Her nails begin to dig into my back, fueling me to go deeper and faster, until the headboard sounds as if it's going to fucking break from banging into the wall.

Fucking let it. It won't be the first time I've had to replace one.

I move up to my knees and grip both of her thighs, lifting her up off the bed so I can fuck her deep like I've been craving since I saw her in the club.

Keeping my grip on her thighs, I grind my hips, pushing as deep as I can to make sure she feels all of me. I want her to feel me everywhere and I'm not stopping until I've had my fill of her. Something tells me it'll be awhile before I'm truly done fucking her.

Growling against her lips, I run my right hand up her body, stopping at her throat. She grips my hand and whimpers as I thrust into her hard, making the headboard bang into the wall.

Then I do it again. And Again. And again, until she screams out as the bed starts to bang against the wall even harder as I fuck her like my life depends on it.

"Want me to stop?" I question against her ear hoping like hell she doesn't tell me yes.

She digs her nails into my arm, telling me to keep going. *Fuck, she's perfect.*

"Shit . . . Lynx," she breathes. "Keep going."

Smirking, I bite her neck and move my hips hard and fast, pounding into her tight, throbbing pussy as if it'll be my last. She wants to fucking play games . . . She's going to feel what I have to offer.

Nipping at her neck and then biting down, I slowly roll my hips into her a few times before resuming my desperate speed.

I roughly suck on her neck to ease the pain of my bites while I continue to move over her. Her grip on me almost hurts as her fingernails pierce my back.

"It's about to break," she pants, while gripping me even harder.

"Good." I thrust into her one more time, hearing it crack where it connects with the bed again. The bed falls with my next thrust and we're both now sliding into the wall. I pull her into my arms and sit back on the bed. She's still wrapped around my waist and I'm still buried deep inside her. She pushes against my chest and I let her think she has control by laying back on the bed.

I can tell by the way her body is shaking above me, that she's about to come at any second, so I grip her face, forcing her to look at me. I want to see her beautiful fucking face as my cock makes her come undone.

She's gorgeous as she rides me. I grip her hips and move her up and down on my cock as I watch her tits bounce and her face flush with my forceful intrusion on a deep thrust I couldn't hold back any longer.

It isn't long and she's moaning through her release, causing me to fly straight into my own, being sure to be as deep as I can as my cum fills the condom.

She collapses against me as I finish and we both breathe deeply until we catch our breath.

"I wasn't supposed to have sex with you." She leans up to look at me, and the sound of her breathy voice makes me happy.

"Who makes these rules of yours? They need to fucking stop." She rolls off of me and I can see she's about to run.

"I do."

"Well stop."

Sure enough, she moves off the bed and starts sliding her clothes on. I just lay there naked and watch her as I remove the condom.

"I know I did this. I also know it's going to get messy if I continue working for you, so consider this my notice. I can't do this."

"Why? You can't handle me giving you orgasms on your breaks?"

"Not funny." She slides on her shoes and I know she's about to bolt. I wish I had it in me to tie her ass up and not let her leave, but I don't.

"I'm serious."

"I am too. Tell me how this is supposed to go. I come to work every day and fight the urge to crawl right back in that bed again while you find it exciting to torture me. Then I'll feel like shit every time I slip. I'll see you with women all the time and it'll make me crazy. I can't deal with that mess. Thank you for the job while it lasted."

"You're not done working here."

"Yes I am."

"No you're not. You have a year."

"I can't work with you for a year. I didn't even make it a week." She's truly upset about this.

"I think you're doing a fantastic job, in fact I think you're due for a promotion." I sit up in the bed and watch her pace the room a few more times.

"Like I said, thank you for the opportunity, but this isn't working." She moves for the door and I feel disappointment wash over me.

"I'll see you tomorrow at nine."

"No you won't." She opens the door and closes me in the room.

I yell out before she makes it very far, "Yes I will!"

Fuck, this woman makes me crazy.

Chapter Fifteen

Rebel

I'M COMPLETELY AND UTTERLY PISSED off at myself for thinking for one second that I would've been able to distract Lynx just enough to give me a ticket out of his little stroke fest with his client so that I could finish my work for the day and get out of there.

All I was hoping for was to annoy him to the point of him wanting to get me out of there so he could finish his damn show in peace.

I never for one second stopped to think that he'd fuck me so damn good that even the idea of going there again has me in a panic.

He made my body feel things that it never even knew were possible. No man has *ever* made me feel so damn good in bed.

How the hell am I supposed to work for someone that has this much power over not just me, but my body?

If I'm completely honest with myself, I haven't stopped thinking about him since walking out the Alpha Mansion door yesterday. My body is craving for his hard and demanding touch.

"I can't go back there, Remi." It's been a day and I'm still standing firm. "You can't just sleep with your boss and then go back to work for him as if nothing happened."

"Of course you can." Remi sits up from tanning in her Cloud Nine chair. "I've done it more than a few times. I don't see why you can't." She laughs.

"What the hell do you find so funny about this, Remi? I'm humiliated and disappointed with myself."

"Because yeah . . . I can definitely see why you can't. Lynx looks like a fucking god and I'm positive he fucks like one too. There's no way I'd be able to pretend that his *huge* dick hasn't been inside of me." She turns to face me. "So, does it still hurt? I bet it hurt so fucking good when he sunk between your legs."

Annoyed with her for acting as if this is some big fucking joke, I roll my eyes and turn over on my stomach. "None of your business. Speak one more word and I'm going to throat punch you. I'm not in the mood."

"Fine," she mumbles. "I'm thinking maybe I *will* just keep that appointment that I made with him last month. Tomorrow is the day, and if he's no longer your boss . . ." She flips over on her stomach too and then knocks my sunglasses off of my head. "Then there's no reason why I shouldn't watch him pleasure himself on camera. I do miss his beautiful cock."

The idea of Remi watching Lynx on camera instantly makes me want to break her computer, but I decide not to give her the pleasure of knowing. "Whatever. Be sure to tell him to stop with the chats, because I won't be responding to any of his messages."

I scream when my chair suddenly tips over, me landing in the grass on my back, with my chair on top of me.

"You're ignoring him completely?"

When I look up, Remi is standing above me with her hands on her hips. "So you tip my chair over because of it? Real mature."

She scrunches her forehead at me. "Every fucking girl on this planet would die to even get one taste of those sexy as sin lips and you ignore him? I'm not having it."

She takes off running into the house.

"Don't you fucking dare?" I yell after her.

"Stop me!"

Pushing my chair away from me, I scramble to my feet and run through the house, stopping at my bedroom door, when I realize that she's locked me out.

"You bitch," I snarl. "Did you seriously just lock me out of my own room?"

"Does the handle turn?"

"No."

"Then yes."

I bang on the door. "Remi. Open the door."

She doesn't respond this time.

"It's not as simple as you think. I don't want to spend my time getting invested in a job just for it all to get ruined because of sex. Don't you dare tell him I'm coming back to work for him. I can't."

She still doesn't respond.

"Would you just unlock the door?"

A few seconds later, I hear the door handle jiggle a bit, so I push the door open to see Remi rushing back over to my bed.

Without saying a word to me, she begins typing on my computer with the biggest smirk I've ever seen on her lips.

"Oh, Blaze," she begins saying what she's typing as she types it. "That's so hot. Now run your hands down that sexy body of yours. Nice and slow, Big Guy."

I rush over to the computer to see Blaze half-naked on the screen, touching himself so damn good that I gulp, while watching him.

"Remi!" I bump her away from the keyboard. "What are you doing?"

"Calling in for my scheduled call with the big, sexy Blaze. What does it look like?"

She pushes me to get back to the keyboard.

> *BadGirl@heart ~ Oh, fuck. I think I just came a little. I'm so wet now. Sooooo wet, Blaze. Now take those briefs off and show me . . .*

She hits send before she can finish the message, knowing that I'm about to kick her ass, before she can finish.

"Under my name? That's not even cool. Bitch, you owe me like five hundred dollars for this call."

"Oh calm down. I paid him for it this morning."

We both look down at the screen just in time to see Blaze smirk and pull the front of his briefs down, exposing his glorious dick to us.

"Holy shit," I say on a sigh. "He's so thick."

"I know, right. Blaze is second in high demand. That should be enough to work Lynx up."

Remembering the fact that Remi is logged on through my name, I slam the computer shut just as Blaze is about to begin stroking himself for us.

"Why did you do that?" I ask in a panic. "Now Lynx is going to think I watched Blaze touch himself. He has access to every call they receive."

"Exactly." She stands up and walks to the door. "Gives him reason to come find you since you refuse to go to him." She smiles. "You're welcome."

"I hate you sometimes. Do you know that?"

She shrugs. "But you love me more so it doesn't matter. Have fun at work tomorrow." The door slams behind her, before

I can argue back.

A few seconds later, my phone buzzes on the nightstand. I pick it up to see a message from an unknown number.

Unknown: You can consider today as a vacation day. I want you here tomorrow by nine. Don't be late.

Me: I already told you. I can't work for you or close to you.

My heart begins racing as I wait for him to respond. As much as I'm trying to stay away from him, I find myself quickly saving his number in my phone.

Lynx: Working for me won't be a problem. Especially, as long as I keep Blaze away from you . . .

"Oh, crap." I for some reason feel guilty at the fact that he thinks it was me watching Blaze, but a part of me hopes it will be enough to make him want to keep his distance from me. Why would he even bother with someone he thinks wants his friend, when he can have anyone he wants? Right.

He can have any willing girl on her knees or in his bed in a second.

Me: Spying on me?

Lynx: I control everything that has to do with my men. I see every fucking thing, Rebel. See you in the morning.

I toss my phone aside and slowly release a breath.

I'm not really sure whether to be relieved or disappointed that he's possibly pissed off at me.

All I can do at this point is have hope that maybe this job will work out after all.

I have to admit that I enjoyed most of the work, up until the point where he asked me to find something that didn't even fucking exist, just to get me where he wanted me.

Tomorrow is hopefully a new start.

Chapter SIXTEEN

Lynx

I'M PISSED THE FUCK OFF because she called Blaze. It just tells me that I pegged her wrong. She's just like all the rest.

"Why did you take that fucking call?" I open his door ready to kick his ass. He's pulling up his jeans just as I do.

"It was a favor for one of my usual calls that she be able to call me from another profile. Is there a problem?" He looks genuinely surprised and I know he has no idea how I feel about Rebel or even that she's one of my callers. Fuck this is a clusterfuck and I need to get some of this aggression out before I kick someone's ass.

"Never mind. I'm hitting the gym." I slam the door and move fast for the house gym, needing to work off some steam and quickly as fuck. It's the best money I spent in the house. I don't have to leave and it gives the guys a chance to stay in ripped shape for their calls.

I try the knob to the gym only to find it locked. Beating on it loudly, I let whoever is behind it know I'm not fucking playing. I need to work out some aggression and if I can't fuck it out of me, I need to work it out of me. The gym is the only other place

I can get in the kind of work I need right now.

Knox opens the door and holds his finger up to quiet me before he points to his laptop. Fuck, he's taking a call. I need a smaller gym for the guys to use for their calls. I can't even hate on his ass right now because he's being creative as he sits back down on the bench and begins to do slow curls in front of the camera.

Knowing I'm not going to get to work it out while he's stroking his dick near me, I close the door and accept that I'm going to have to go to my last plan of attack. Running.

I fucking hate running, but right now it's all I have to work some of this out.

My mind fills with thoughts of her and the way we've been together the past few days, the entire time I let the music flow through my ear buds. She was fun while she lasted. Shit.

I keep running through the neighborhood and back around the lake. When I get near the boardwalk, I slow to a jog to avoid the people in my path.

It isn't until I see Rebel walking in a bikini that I come to a halting stop. She's walking with another woman in a bikini and they're both talking to each other very expressively.

Walking behind them, I pull out my ear buds when I get close enough to possibly hear them.

"Will you fucking stop talking about fucking your boss. I swear you're literally sitting where every woman in the world would like to be and you're the idiot that can't fucking do it."

"Remi stop yelling. I don't need everyone hearing my business. What the hell." She turns to look around and sees me following them. I take a few steps toward them before I replace my earbuds and begin jogging again, passing them up.

The heat on my back the entire way down the boardwalk tells me she's watching me the whole way.

Their words play through my mind and I continue to let her mindfuck me even after I swore her off.

She's obviously still talking about me, but if she's already making calls to one of my guys, I must not have made that big of an impression.

Once I hit my property, I head straight for the pool to cool off. Sweat is literally dripping from my body as I kick off my shoes to dive into the pool.

I come up for breath only to see a powerful figure standing over me and find Blaze standing there with his arms crossed.

"Hey Boss, how's it going?"

"I'm hanging in there. How about you?" I slide out of the pool and sit on the edge while he starts to talk.

"My twin brother, Luca, needs a job. Do you think he could come in and take one of those spare rooms?" I'm surprised to hear he has a twin.

"Fuck, you have a twin. Why did I not know this?"

"I don't share shit. You know this."

"If you think he's cut out for it, we can definitely let him in for a trial to see if it works out, but it worries my ass to think of there being two of you. I hope like fuck I can handle it."

"He's nothing like me. Alright. Thanks." Just then Rome walks up to join him standing over me.

"How's it going?" Blaze speaks to Rome first.

"Whose ass am I billing for taking my cross?" I smile, finally realizing that Rome is going to be the full blown Dom in the house with all the BDSM furniture.

"Yeah. Sorry about that." I have to fess up. "Bill me and I'll get you covered."

"I'm not taking calls for a few days until I get my playroom ready. I think it'll be a good addition to the kind of calls I can take. Plus, I'm always up for that kinky shit." He starts to walk away.

"I should've known it was yours. Let me know when your twin arrives, Blaze. I want to meet him before we make it official."

"I'll let you know when he's headed this way. It'll be a couple weeks."

They both walk away and I let my mind start thinking about the shit he can do with a set up like that. It's genius and the exact reason I wanted the guys all together in one house.

They feed off each other and will work to one up the other guys. Hell, I'm feeling myself stepping up to the plate more with these guys in my face with their innovative ideas.

I sit and think about where everything is headed for me. The last thing I need is Rebel to complicate my life by being here every day. Seeing her today at the beach instantly had my dick reacting and if I'm going to really make this company grow, I need to remove any distractions that would hinder me.

I grab my phone and dial the club.

"Hey Brit, call Rebel in to work at the club tonight. Schedule her every night for at least a week."

"Damn, Boss. She must've pissed you off."

"She said something about needing money."

"Yeah, alright. I'll give her the VIP section if that's alright with you?"

"Do what you want, you and Envy are the ones running it." I'm about to hang up when she starts talking again.

"I heard you had one hell of a party a few nights ago."

"How'd you hear?" I ask, annoyed.

"Blaze was telling me." That fucker and his mouth. I need to tell him to keep the club business separate from the house.

"Yeah, it was intense," I say, leaving out the details. "Next time, extend me an invite. I'd love to chill with you guys one night." Brit has no idea what we do here. I've purposely made it that way. At least I don't think she's seen what we do. Who knows. Hell she could be one of my regular callers as far as I know.

"Yeah. Maybe one of these days. Alright. I'll see you tomorrow for our meeting. Until then, keep the club shit going for me. I'll compensate you well, I promise. I hope to have you some management help in there soon."

"You'd better. Don't get me wrong, I love this place, but a girl can only take so many nights of this shit in a row."

"I can only imagine. Talk to you later." And with that, I end the call.

There. Rebel won't be a distraction for me now. I won't have her near me to remind me how she fucking feels. How she fucking tastes. How she fucking fucks. Damn it. Just the thought of her pisses me off all over again.

"I need a damn shower." I talk to myself as I move across the room, stripping off my clothes as I do. I take the longest shower of my life and just let the water wash over me.

Stepping out, I hear the guys getting louder downstairs. I'm sure they're doing their normal rowdy get together as usual and I find myself looking forward to being in the middle of all of that. It'll get my mind right if I'm with the guys.

When I get near my phone, I hear a message come in.

> *Rebel: I just want you to know it was my friend who called Blaze on the chat line, but I agree it's best if I just work at the club for now. Thanks for a great time while it lasted.*

She's making me fucking insane. One minute she can't handle being around me, the next she thanks me for a great time. I'm getting whiplash from her indecisiveness.

It does make me feel better that she wasn't the one calling

Blaze, calming me down some.

I finally put my phone away after a few minutes, deciding not to respond to her right now. I have too much shit on my mind.

And with that I open my bedroom door to hear the guys yelling even louder.

"I'm not getting my damn dick stabbed. What the fuck is wrong with you people?" Blaze is yelling over all of the other guys in the room.

"You damn pussy. It's just a piercing."

"Fuck off! I'm not doing that shit." I look over the railing to see them all on the first floor below me. He's walking away from them holding his dick like it hurts him to think about it.

"I'm gonna bet you will. The piercer will be here tonight. It's my little contribution to the house meeting." Knox is pestering the shit out of Blaze and it brings a smile to my face.

"Count me in." I look over to Knox and let him know I'm in for this little get together. Dick piercings have always intrigued me. I'll try anything once.

"Awesome. Pussy over there isn't up for it. Has his nipples pierced, but won't do his cock."

"Eh. Leave him bare. The women will lose their shit when we all get pierced. It just means more business for the rest of us," Rome chimes in causing all of us to bust out laughing.

"Tempt me all you want, assholes. I'm not letting someone stab my dick. I actually use mine every day, unlike the rest of you." Blaze flops down on the couch and throws his leg over the arm of it.

I stand back and look at all the guys interacting. This is the kind of energy I had hoped would come with having them all live under the same roof.

This is something I can get used to.

Chapter SEVENTEEN

Lynx

THE BODY PIERCER SHOWED UP twenty minutes ago and Blaze's ass hasn't come out of his room since he heard the fucking doorbell ring.

He took off, still complaining about his dick getting stabbed.

"Come out you fucking pussy!" Rome shouts, before tossing back a shot of whiskey and dropping his pants for Karma.

Blaze is going to kick himself in the dick later when he realizes the body piercer is a hot as fuck blazing redhead with facial piercings and tattoos. She has a nose piercing, her upper cheek and a sexy as hell Monroe piercing. This chick looks pretty fucking badass.

I know Blaze's type and she fits it to a T.

Knowing that I need to get his ass out here, I leave the room right as Rome reaches for a shirt and stuffs it in his mouth.

"Stop being a pussy and come out, fucker."

Blaze pops his head out the door. "I told you. I'm not letting some chick stab a needle through my dick."

I nod for him to join me by the railing. "Your loss. You're going to be kicking your own ass later when you're the only one in the house without one."

He's hesitant at first, but walks a few feet to peer over the railing. "Holy fuck!" He grabs his dick and adjusts it. "If she's going to be handling my cock, sign my ass up."

"I figured you'd say that shit. You're after Nash."

Picking his balls up, he rushes down the stairs as if his dick is on fire. I'm not so sure I've ever seen his ass move so fast.

By the time we get downstairs, Rome is chillin' with his new piercing and Nash is getting into position next.

Nash is calm and cool since he's had this done once before and knows what to expect. He drops his pants and whips out his cock for her. "Give me the Double Dydoe."

Karma eyes his cock and quickly sterilizes before inserting the first needle through.

Nash squeezes his eyes shut, but barely moves a muscle as she moves on to the second one.

"Stop showing off, asshole. There's got to be something wrong with your dick if that shit didn't hurt."

"Never said it didn't hurt." Nash winks at Karma and then looks down to admire her work. "Damn, the ladies are going to love the hell out of me."

"Fuck!"

Blaze draws Karma's attention to him when he starts to panic. She smirks, realizing that she has someone new joining the group. "You must be my next victim. Drop your pants, Gorgeous."

"Fuck! What am I doing?" Blaze drops his pants, but keeps his boxer briefs up.

Karma looks down at the bulge in his briefs, before reaching out and pulling them down. Her eyes widen as she takes in his size. "Alright, Babe. What kind of piercing do you want? Prince Albert, Jacob's Ladder, Dolphin, Ampallang, Apadravya, Frenum,

Lorum . . ."

She starts naming off the piercings and I can feel my dick already beginning to hurt. Blaze must feel it too, because he's already beginning to sweat.

"Holy fuck! There's that many?"

Karma places her hands on Blaze's chest and pushes him down, until he's lying on the couch. "You scared, Big Guy?" She flashes a fierce smile and snaps her gloves on. "Just think of how pretty your dick will look after I'm done."

"Pretty enough for you to wrap your sexy ass lips around it?" he challenges. "I'll let you do anything you want to it then, Beautiful."

She roughly grabs his dick and positions him how she wants it. "Anything I want to it, Playboy?"

He looks down at his cock that is pretty much completely hard now. "Fuck me!"

She licks her lips. "You're nice and big . . . I'm thinking a Jacob's ladder."

"Do it!" Nash yells. "Give this pretty darlin' what she wants."

"Do you really have to be fucking hard right now?" I throw a pillow at his head. "Just man up."

He nervously runs his hands over his face. "I'm trusting your beautiful ass with my cock. Take care of it. I'm fucking begging you."

She smiles while getting her equipment ready. "I'll take *real* good care of it, baby. Especially since you begged. I like that in a man."

The whole room laughs when Blaze grips the edge of the couch and begins shouting random cuss words as she pushes the first needle through without warning.

"It's sometimes better not to know when it's coming." She looks around the room and smiles. "Your dick's still hard . . . must not hurt too bad."

Turning away from the chaos of Blaze and his dick, I pull out my phone to see another message from Rebel. She sent it about ten minutes ago.

> *Rebel: We need to talk about this job. Is there any way of getting out of that contract?*

"Shit," I say to myself.

"Everything good?" Knox asks from beside me, while pulling his dark hair out of his face.

"Yeah. Nothing I can't handle."

Before I know it, Karma has Blaze all cleaned up and waiting for me to step up.

"Looks like the boss is next," Karma teases. She's trying her best to keep her eyes off Blaze's dick, but I see her eyes traveling back to him as she prepares the new equipment.

Not hesitating too much and overthinking it, I drop my pants and take my spot on the couch, after Blaze wipes the leather clean.

Karma seems impressed as she looks down at me, ready for her to stab my damn dick and get it over it.

"Very nice." She lifts a brow. "What would you like me to grace your dick with?"

The buzzer at the gate goes off, distracting me for a moment. "Rome. Go check it out."

"Got it, Boss." Rome jumps up and runs over to the screen, before letting whoever it is in the gate.

Ignoring the rest of the room, I think about what might be the best piercing to pleasure Rebel. Fuck! She has me all fucked up.

"Fuck." I pump myself up. "Give me the Apa."

She smirks down at me. "Good choice."

Closing my eyes, I take a deep breath and growl out as she pushes the needle through.

"Oh my God!"

I open my eyes to the sound of Rebel's voice.

She's standing next to Rome, looking down at my dick. Her eyes roam from my new piercing, over to Blaze who still hasn't covered up and then back over to me again. She looks a little jealous when Karma grabs my dick to clean it off.

"This is probably not the best time for me to be here." She turns around and begins heading for the door with a quickness. "I just came to discuss work. Get back to me when you can."

"Stay," I demand. "We're going to discuss this now. And to answer your text. No."

Rebel watches me with curious eyes as I stand up and pull my sweats up, being sure that the fabric doesn't touch my dick.

"Your dick looks like it might hurt. It's probably not the best time to discuss business. I'm going."

Rome wraps his arm around Rebel's neck and leans in close to her ear, being sure to brush up against her. "My piercing is better than his. Just a heads up."

"Fuck off, Rome. Hands off," I say tensely, my blood now boiling at his closeness. "Meet me in my office. I'll be there in five minutes."

She looks hesitant, but walks up the stairs anyway.

"Whoa." Blaze looks down at his dick. "This shit does make my dick look pretty fucking sweet."

Not wanting to deal with any of these fuckers and their dicks right now, I thank Karma and throw her a hundred-dollar tip.

Once I get upstairs to my office, I close the door and strip out of my pants, so I'm standing here completely naked now.

"Let's talk."

Rebel turns around at the sound of my voice and her mouth completely drops as she looks me over with my new piercing.

It's making it so fucking hard that I won't be able to use it on her for a while. I want to feel her heavy breath as she screams against my lips. That will have to wait.

Fuck, I need to make sure she doesn't leave . . .

❦

Rebel

MY EYES WANDER OVER HIS body, taking in every hard inch of muscle, including the newly pierced one that is now standing at full alert.

Fuck, it just made him even hotter.

How am I supposed to discuss this issue with him when he's standing there looking so damn sexy and irresistible?

"Can you put your pants back on, please?"

"Not a chance."

He comes at me, picking me up and setting me on the edge of his desk. Leaning in against my ear, he spreads my knees with his leg and steps between my legs. "Is it true?" he questions against my ear, his lips gently brushing my skin.

He's so damn close that I can't even think. What?

"Is what true?"

Gripping my hair, he tugs and pulls my head back to press kisses along my neck. "That it was your friend that called Blaze?"

I swallow and grip the desk as I feel his teeth graze my flesh. It's such a damn turn on. "Does it really matter?" I stammer.

Growling, he grips my hair harder and breathes heavily against my neck. "Fuck yes."

His erection pokes me between the legs. I inhale a breath, imagining what it would be like to have him take me right here on his desk with his newly pierced dick.

"I wouldn't lie," I admit. "There's no reason for me to call anyone but you." It slips out before I can stop it. Not that he needed to know that.

"Fuck." He wraps his hand around my throat. "That's all I needed to hear."

With that, he presses his lips against mine, kissing me so damn hard that he knocks the breath right out of my lungs.

Even his kisses are full of control and demand. He's so damn Alpha and sexy.

The more his kiss deepens, the faster my heart begins to beat against his chest. My hands reach out to grip his hair and I find myself wrapping my legs around his waist, wanting nothing more than to get as close to him as humanly possible.

"Don't quit," he whispers against my lips. "I want you here, but I can't promise you that I'll keep my hands to myself."

"I can't promise either," I say while fighting to catch my breath.

"Boss!" One of the guys yells, while banging on the door. "We need your ass out here."

"Fuck!" Lynx looks completely pissed, like he wants to wring someone's neck. "Fuck you guys and you always banging on the door. I'm about to cut your hands off."

"I'd still use my dick."

"Blaze . . . you motherfucker."

Gripping my hair with both hands, Lynx presses another kiss against my lips, biting my bottom lip as he pulls away. "I want you here tomorrow morning. Fuck working at the bar for the week."

Unable to form any words, I just nod my head and watch as

he grabs his sweats and holds them against his front side as he walks out the door.

So much for quitting . . .

Chapter EIGHTEEN

Rebel

IT TAKES EVERY OUNCE OF restraint not to go to work early. Working the shift at the club yesterday only verified that I missed working near him. He always has me on my toes and to be honest, he's hot as fuck and even though I've given myself a thousand reasons I shouldn't work for him, I always come back to the chemistry between us.

I've never felt the fire that I feel around him. He burns me up and I'm finding myself craving his intensity every time I'm not near him. Besides, I'm pretty sure Remi would kill me if I don't at least have some fun with Lynx before I walk away.

Pulling into the gate, I don't even have to say my name today. The attendant must know me by now and it makes me smile to know that Lynx probably told him to let me in any time I want in.

When I drive up to the house, I see the guys out front all standing in their underwear.

"Let me adjust my shit so you can see my new metal through these tight fuckers." Blaze has his hands in his pants as he's focused on perfectly positioning his bulge. I try not to notice, but the truth is, I do.

Lynx sees me step out of my Jeep and moves toward me quickly. "Hey. We're just doing a shoot here for a few minutes. The piercer is going to use us as advertisement and I plan to use this for our website too. It's fucking genius."

"It is. I'll just go in and get started on that paperwork you started to show me the other day." I look at him nervously as he stands in his red underwear.

"It's nice to know you still like what you see." He moves in close to me, practically rubbing against me as he moves me until I'm leaning against the side door of my Jeep.

"God, you're fucking sexy. Do you know how *hard* it's been trying not to call you?" He accentuates the *hard* and I know what he's trying to say.

"I can only imagine." He slides his hands up my arms just before the guys begin to yell obscenities at us.

"Yeah buddy! Fuck her right on the hood of her Jeep. Let Big Daddy see you in action."

Lynx smiles and yells back without ever turning away from looking at me. "Shut the fuck up, Blaze." He pulls away slowly, leaving some type of oil on my shirt. "You'll never see me with her."

Before he walks away, he takes one step closer to me again to whisper in my ear. "You know my dick is still hard from standing close to you last night. I think I'm going to have to try this new piercing out on you soon."

"About that. We need to talk before anything more happens."

"Shit. No rules. I'm not listening to any fucking rules, so decide what you have to say and I'll decide what I want to hear." I take in his forceful response and have to laugh. I don't know if he's sexually frustrated with me or just annoyed that I keep putting the brakes on every time he tries to do anything.

"I'll see you inside in a few minutes. Until then, think about my dick some more."

"Excuse me?" Why am I surprised at his confidence?

"Don't pretend you haven't been thinking about it. In fact..." He grabs my hand and places my fingers on his lips. "I'm guessing you thought about me late last night when you dipped these into that sweet fuckin' pussy of yours." My face must turn red, because his laughter is obnoxious as he finally walks away.

Damn him for being able to see through me.

There's no way he could tell by kissing my fingers, he just assumed and fucking hell he was right. I mean, I did shower and wash my hands multiple times before I came here this morning.

"You don't know." I try to save face a little with a poor excuse for a response to his comment.

"I bet I do." He'll challenge me all day if I don't get out of here. He knows how to keep me on edge, that's for sure.

I walk through the front door to the house to find a major mess from the night before. It's obvious they all just stayed around here and consumed everything in sight. Food and bottles are all over the place.

I'm straightening the kitchen when they all walk into the house.

"What are you doing?" Lynx moves into the kitchen, quickly stopping me from putting more bottles in the trash.

"Just picking up a little."

"No. The guys can get their own shit picked up. You're not their damn housekeeper," he says loud enough for the house to hear.

"It's no big deal. Seriously."

"Yes it fucking is. If you do this today, they'll think you'll do it every damn day. Guys get your shit picked up. She's not your fuckin' maid." He pulls a bottle from my hand and throws it into the trash can.

"Come to my office and I'll get you started for the day." I follow him through the main entrance and up the stairs to his office. He closes the door behind me and pulls me back against his body.

"We still have to talk. I want to do this right this time and please let me set some boundaries."

"Fuck boundaries. There should be nothing between us."

"Ok. Seriously, sit down and let's do this correctly." I walk toward his desk and point to his chair, trying to convince him to at least go along with this.

His smile spreads even wider on his face when I start to get demanding.

"I like when you're bossy."

"No. Sit and have a real business conversation with me. I need you to really listen to me." He sits and scoots his chair back so I have a view of his bulge covered in red just over the desk. Damn, he's not playing fair. I let my eyes brush over his tattoos before I begin to talk.

"I need boundaries. It's important to me that I earn my paycheck. I'm not fucking you to get paid."

"I can live with that." He sets his elbow on the armrest of his chair and then begins to run his hand over his short beard while he watches me closely.

"Work hours are work hours. You need to respect that I'm not coming here to fuck you every day. If you want more out of me, you have to spend time with me outside of working hours." He lifts his eyebrows as I continue to talk.

"And you don't get to talk to me all dirty when I'm working."

"No deal. That's what I do," he growls, while looking me over as if that's what he wants to do right this second.

"Lynx. I don't expect this to turn into anything more than

just some playful time with you. I know you'll move on to your many women and I'll be ok with that. That's why I want us to set up some professionalism in this. I deserve to have that from you. Besides from the looks of it, you actually really need help with this business."

"I do need help. The admin shit is killing me."

"I can help with that if you let me, but I won't let you make me feel like I'm just getting paid to spread my legs for you whenever you want."

"Are you done making rules yet? Because I'm done listening. I'm not paying you to fuck me. Shit, people pay me to see my dick on the daily. I don't have to pay for a damn thing. I sincerely will have you working here to help me with the shit we talked about, but I'm not promising that I'll be able to keep my hands off of you and I'm sure as fuck not promising that I'll keep the filthy shit from coming out of my mouth." He stands up and walks to my side of the desk. He sits on the edge of it, giving me an eye level view of his cock in those underwear.

I fight the urge to reach up and run my fingers up his abs and over his chest.

"Can you at least try to keep it to a minimum? And one more thing. Don't accept a call with me in the room. I don't want to see that unless I'm the one making the call."

"Alright then, you have to promise me that you'll take a call from me when I call you." I stand and look him in the eyes. Something tells me all of this is just the beginning of me making a few bad decisions, but I nod in agreement.

"Where should I get started today?" He grabs my hand and sets it on his dick; keeping his over mine, he pushes against my hand.

I can feel him getting hard with the next firm grip he makes with my hand under his.

"Start here." He softly moans when I squeeze my fingers into his growing erection.

"Lynx. I told you after hours. I'm here to work." He holds my hand tighter against his bulge and begins to breathe harder.

"Taking care of my dick can be your job. It needs to be moisturized before I get on camera."

"Here we are again. So quickly right where we started." I have to point out to him that we're back to square one.

"I know, it's great." He steps forward and brushes my hair way from my face. "I'm going to try to find a boundary with you, but it's not going to be today. It might not even be tomorrow." He kisses my cheek before he slides his lips over mine.

"It's going to take me a little while to get you out of my system. Then I might be able to comprehend these boundaries you speak of." He lowers his underwear, then moves my hand back over his cock.

"Be careful with it. It's still sore." I look down and admire his piercing. He has an Apa. It's known to hit a G-spot if done right. I used to date a tattoo artist who also did piercings. It was one he actually didn't have so I've never felt one during sex.

"How can you even be thinking about sex after that?" I ask softly, unable to stop looking at how hot it looks on him.

"How could I not?" He's still rubbing against me and I can tell he's horny as hell, even if his dick is sore from the fresh piercing.

"Can you even do anything with that for six weeks?"

"Fuck the rules." He pulls a condom from a small box on his desk and rolls it over his length, slowly. "Sit on my desk."

"We didn't even make it five minutes, Lynx."

"Sure we did. Slide your pants down first and then get up there and spread those beautiful legs for me. I need this. Right. Fucking. Now." I follow his commands and watch as he grips my hips, slowly sliding his cock into me. I can feel him inch by fucking inch.

We both moan as he works it in more with each thrust, giving me time to adjust to his size first. He pushes me slowly until my back is flat against the desk. His grip on my hips is tight as he pulls me toward him repeatedly, only to release a low growl each time he slams into me.

When he's finally all the way in, he slams into me hard and instantly sends me screaming into an orgasm as he does it over and over again, fucking me as if to show me that no one else will ever feel this damn good. I have a feeling that he's right.

He doesn't stop even when I'm trying to back away from him, while gripping at anything that I can reach. Before I know it, my body begins to tremble and then he's moving his fingers over my clit at a fast pace, making me scream even louder as I squirt for the first time in my life. It's so damn intense that I can barely handle the sensation.

"Hell yes. I'm going to fucking love this piercing." He continues to fuck me through my sensitive come down and before I know it, I'm on the rise again.

"Shit. So good." I'm not even sure what I'm saying as he finishes driving into me the last few times before he squirms through his own release, digging his teeth into my neck.

"Fuck. What have you done to me?" He leans over me before he kisses my neck where he just bit it. I can't believe how sexual this man is. He's been great every time I've been with him, even when we didn't go all the way.

I think the real question is, what has he done to me?

Chapter Nineteen

Lynx

REBEL MUST BE FUCKING CRAZY to think that I can go longer than five minutes without wanting to devour every inch of her beautiful body.

The fucked up thing is that I can usually control myself when it comes to women. Not when it comes to her. My dick actually aches at just the thought of her being near, not to mention the fact that it's still throbbing from fucking her while the tip is still sore. I must be fucked up, because I actually liked the torture of how it felt every time I hit her deep. *Shit, I need to stop thinking about my dick.*

I've left her alone in the office for four hours now. I'm trying my hardest to respect her wishes, but I can tell right now that it's not going to be easy to wait until *after* work hours.

As far as I know, she's wrapping up schedules and payments now and then she'll be heading out for the day.

This shouldn't bother me, but fuck. I want more time with her.

Poking my head through the office door, I catch her stacking up a pile of papers and shoving them into the cabinet. She's oblivious to me watching her, so I take a few minutes to take her in while she works.

She's so damn beautiful and doesn't even know it. I know without a doubt that every one of my guys would jump at the opportunity to make her theirs. Not fucking happening.

Placing her hand over her chest, she lets out a small scream when she turns around to see me watching her. "Shit, Lynx. How long have you been there?"

I smile and step into the office. "Just long enough to see how fucking beautiful you are while you're lost in concentration."

Her cheeks redden as she looks me over, trying her hardest not to look down at my dick that is now completely fucking hard again. "I was just finishing up for the day. Anything else you want done before I leave?"

I step up next to her and wrap both of my hands into her hair, letting my eyes trail down to her plump lips. "No, but you can come with me to *Club Royal* tonight."

She sucks in a small breath and grips my arms as I begin trailing kisses up her neck, stopping just below her ear. "I want to spend time with you outside of work. Fuck, I don't just want you then, Rebel." I trail one hand down her body, stopping on her ass as I whisper in her ear. "I want you so much more than you know and more than I can even begin to figure out."

A small moan escapes her parted lips as I give her ass a squeeze. "What time? I have a little work to do first," she breathes out.

Pulling her closer, I press my erection into her. "I'll pick you up by nine."

She laughs. "You don't have my address."

She's fucking crazy if she doesn't think I know where she lives. I keep her file in close reach. Perks of being the boss. "Sure I do."

Her eyes come up to meet mine and the way she's looking into them as if she's trying to see what's inside, I get the sudden urge to slam my lips against hers and claim them again.

I want to lick them, suck them and bite them. Anything to show her that they're mine.

"You surprise me."

"How so?" I question, while running my thumb over her bottom lip.

"You intimidate me, yet make me feel completely wanted and safe at the same time. I never know what to expect from your mouth, but it has the same effect on me every time. And your eyes . . ." she stops and smiles. "They give you away and I guess that's what surprises me. What your eyes have to say."

I smile, not really knowing what she's getting at. Maybe they give more away than I thought. "I wish your eyes would give more away," I respond.

We both stand here looking at each other, until the office door pushes further open and Nash pops his head inside. "Boss. You have a call waiting on you. I have Rome's ass trying to hold them off until you get there."

"Fuck!" I didn't even realize I had a call scheduled for today. I only have my damn self to blame for not letting Rebel do her work the other day. "On my way. Rome better not have his cock whipped out in my room and touching my shit."

Nash shrugs. "Couldn't tell ya. Better hurry."

Rebel backs away from me and clears her throat. "I'll just clean up and get out of here. Enjoy your call."

"Shit," I mumble to myself. Talk about shitty timing. "I'll see you tonight. Be ready by nine."

Growling under my breath, I take off down the hall in a hurry. If I leave Rome alone for too long in my room, his ass will probably have his dick touching everything in sight.

When I make it to my room, Rome is grinding against the arm of my leather couch like a damn stripper, while pulling down the front of his underwear to show her the base of his cock. He grinds his hips a few more times, before whipping his cock out and slowly running his hand over its length.

"Holy shit, Rome. Why haven't I called you yet? You're young and absolutely delicious. That body and the way you move . . ."

I stand back and look at the screen to see one of my regulars. @Prettygirl84 is one of the clients that has shown her face from the very first call. She's extremely hot and dirty. Before Rebel, she was my favorite caller.

Seeing how much she's enjoying Rome actually makes me happy that I hired him.

Biting his bottom lip, Rome looks my way and nods his head at me, before turning back to the screen and releasing his dick. "Lynx is ready." He covers his cock back up and grabs his jeans, picking them up. "Schedule a call with me and I'll be happy to show you what dirty means."

"Oh my goodness." My client bites her bottom lip and runs a hand over her breasts and watches as Rome walks past me and bumps his fist with mine.

"Thanks for entertaining my client. I'll send some money your way to make up for it."

He just smiles and nods his head, before jogging out of my room and leaving me alone with @Prettygirl84.

"Damn, Lynx. Rome warmed me up pretty good while waiting on you. I'm already close. My undies are off and my pussy is throbbing."

This used to excite me with her, but for some fucked up reason, I don't feel shit. In fact, I'm still thinking about how I buried myself in Rebel this morning.

"Rome *is* one of my guys. I only take the best." I watch as she takes her bra off and squeezes one of her breasts. "How do you want me to finish you off?"

"Mmmm . . ." she moans. "You know how I want you to finish me off, Lynx. With your humongous dick inside of me, pounding into me through all hours of the night. I'm so damn wet. I'll take you and Rome at the same time. One in each hole."

"Holy fuck. Someone's extra dirty today."

Not waiting for her command, I step out of my jeans and lay back on my leather couch, rubbing my hand over my erection.

She may think this is for her and I'll continue to let her believe it. It's what keeps them coming back.

I'm no longer watching her on the screen as I whip my cock out and begin stroking it with both hands. She's only got five minutes left of her call and even though I'm not into this right now, there's no way I'm not making sure she gets off before this call ends.

Closing my eyes, I give it my all as I remember the way Rebel squirted this morning. From her reaction, I can tell it was her first.

"These new piercings are doing me in," she moans. "I can't handle it. Oh fuck! It's so hot. Keep going."

My speed picks up at the mention of my piercing. Rebel loved the way it felt inside of her pussy and I can't wait to make her come again.

"Faster," she begs.

I speed up and within seconds, I hear *@Prettygirl84* moan louder than I've ever heard from her before. She's panting so damn hard that you would think I was physically there fucking her.

"So good . . ." she moans. "I came so damn hard."

Pulling my boxer briefs back up, I stand up and walk over to the screen. "Sorry I was late. From the sound of you screaming, I'll take it that you still had a good time."

She smiles and leans back in her chair, completely naked with her legs spread. Even through the computer I can see just how wet she is. "It was so damn good. Next time you can warn a girl before showing up with some piercings. I came harder than I ever have before."

I can see the time counting down on the screen so I thank her for her call and quickly disconnect to get my head straight.

All I can think about is what I'm going to do with Rebel once I get her to the club tonight. It almost feels like a fucking date. I don't do dates. Never have.

But that doesn't stop me from wanting to make sure she has a good time with me.

I guess there's a first time for everything . . .

Chapter TWENTY

Rebel

"HE'S GOING TO BE HERE in like twenty minutes. You need to hurry!" Remi is driving me crazy with her excitement about my evening plans. I can't call this a date, because something tells me he wouldn't go for that kind of thing.

I'm looking forward to tonight no matter what he wants to call it. There's no doubt I'll be on the edge of my seat waiting to see what his next move will be. I'm curious to see if he'll be the same with me in a public place as he has been since the party. The thought of that frightens me just a little. He's so intense, but honestly that's what draws me to him.

The doorbell rings before I'm finished putting my heels on and I can hear Remi talking in the background. Something tells me she's going to say something embarrassing, but me being in the room wouldn't change that either. I would just be there to hear it, so I may as well let her do her thing before I go in.

I take one last look at my dress in the mirror and see a panty line. "Shit. That has to go." I lift my dress and start to slide my panties down, deciding to go for a lacy thong instead. Just then the bathroom door opens and I look over to see him watching me.

"What are you doing? Do you not understand the concept of knocking?"

"If I would've knocked, I would've missed this view." I hurry to pull my tight dress down over my hips, trying to save some sense of privacy. Which is ridiculous since he's seen every single inch of my body in the past few days.

"Seriously, you really need to learn some boundaries, Lynx." He's against my back, pulling my ass into his hips before I have the chance to finish my sentence.

"When it comes to you, I can't help myself. I was hoping I'd catch you doing something sexy, and baby, you sure as fuck didn't disappoint." He spreads his hands wider over my hips and then begins to move them slowly across my body. His touch flows through me, instantly causing me to crave him even more.

"I like how you're not wearing anything under this sexy as fuck dress. It lets me know I have access when I can't stand it another second." He's grinding against me as one of his hands covers my chest and the other one slides up my dress and between my legs. He slides a finger over my clit and I work not to respond to him like my body wants to.

"I'm just changing them." I'm all breathy sounding, even though I'm trying like hell not to be.

"No you're not. I'll just rip them off." I look at him in the mirror and see the seriousness in his eyes.

Why is he so damn sexy? His dark hair is perfect. The scruff on his face makes me want to rub my legs together as I remember how it felt between my legs.

His tattoos are peeking out through the sleeve of his black shirt and I just want to rub my fingers over each and every one of them.

He turns me around to face him and then lifts me up onto

the bathroom counter. He moves between my legs as he pulls my lips toward his.

His kiss is aggressive at first and I follow his lead, allowing him to pull my lip between his teeth before I do the same to him. His low growl encourages me to continue moving my hands until I'm holding his ass in both of them.

"We're never going to leave here. Feel my cock trying like hell to get to you? I'm going to bust the fuck out of these jeans."

"Is this all you want me for?" I reach to feel his bulge and smile knowing it's only making it more difficult to walk out of here.

"No. It's just everything about you goes straight to my dick. What can I say? I really like what I see." He continues to kiss me while he pulls me closer, lifting me around his waist.

He walks us both into my room just in time for Remi to walk by and see us. The smile on her face is ridiculous and of course she doesn't just walk on by.

"Holy fuck, you two are hot. I'm gonna get my stuff and leave you to it. Don't mind me." She closes the door and I have to laugh. She's such a pain in my ass, but I love her to pieces.

I know she has her own date tonight and I'm actually surprised she's still here. There's no doubt in my mind she wanted to make sure she met Lynx in person. I mean, it is Remi we're talking about here.

He continues to carry me to the door of my bedroom. I start to slide down his body thinking we're about to leave only to have him stop me.

"I can almost feel your hot pussy against my cock. It's not even right that we leave before I get to actually feel it." He presses me against the door and starts rubbing in all the perfect places.

"Shit. I can still hear you!" Remi yells from the other side of the door and I bust out laughing.

"So leave unless you want to hear more!" Lynx yells back just before he begins to kiss me again. He continues for a few seconds, slowly rubbing his hands on my body again. I use my legs and arms to hold myself on him.

"We should leave if you really want to go somewhere tonight. Otherwise, I'm good with staying here or we can even go back to my house if you just want to play." He talks with such a deep voice and seriousness that I almost make a move to get him to stay. I know for a fact it would only take a slight move on my part for him to get my signal and take me up on an offer to just fuck all night long.

He sets me down and I quickly think to myself how ridiculous I am for not jumping straight back to sex with this guy, but it would be nice to know we have more than just sexual chemistry between us.

"We can leave, but you can't put on panties. I want to know you're bare for me." I walk to my panty drawer and pull out a pair to slide over my legs.

"Put them on and I promise it'll be the last time you get to wear them." Looking back at him, I can tell he's not joking, but I've never done anything like this in public in a dress.

"Lynx. Stop. I'm wearing these and you'll be fine knowing I'm wearing this sexy lace and if you're lucky, I'll let you take them off of me." I sit on the edge of my bed and start to slide them over my heels. I even let him get a peek of what he's hoping to see as I move to the next leg.

"Are you trying to kill me?" He begins to move for me again.

"No. Just trying to keep up with your games you like to play." I stand before he gets to me, then walk away from him to turn off my bathroom light. He's right behind me when I stop.

"You can play all you fucking want. In fact, it turns me the fuck on. But I will demolish that lace before the night's over. I hope you enjoy wearing them one last time." I swallow when his deep voice sets so close to my ear. He screams sexual tension and it's not fair that he can make me turn into this mush of a mess that I am when he's near me.

"If you rip these, then I'll bill your ass to replace them." I say with confidence knowing this will in no way deter him from ripping them off of me.

"Fine. Add about forty pair to the bill when you do. That should get us through a few weeks." He smiles before he kisses me one last time. His hands cover my ass and he squeezes just as he pulls away.

"Alright. Let's get the fuck out of here before it's too late. I can't take much more of this." He opens the door to my bedroom and we both step out into the main living room just in time to hear Remi drive away.

"Nice place you guys have here." He starts to make small talk while I finish turning off the lights.

"Thanks. Remi and I are trying to make it as nice as possible." We step outside and I stop in my tracks when I see he brought a motorcycle to pick me up.

"Is that what we're taking?" I ask, knowing it's a silly question.

He begins to walk toward it. "Yep."

I look down at my dress and quickly turn to unlock the door. "There's no way in hell I can ride on that in this dress. My ass would be out the entire time." And to think he wanted me without panties.

"Sure you can. It'll be sexy as fuck to have you riding with me like that."

"Not a chance in hell. Why didn't you tell me I'd need to change when you saw me?" He's following me back in.

"Because you don't need to. You look fucking phenomenal.

If it'll make you feel better, we'll drive yours." I contemplate it, but decide I probably need to change. I'm not sure what he'll have me doing tonight and the last thing I should probably be is unprepared.

"Give me a few minutes and I'll change." I grab a pair of jeans and a tight top to go along with what he's wearing. He gives me space to change and I even leave out the panties just to make this an even trade. He can find that I compromised later, if he's lucky.

If I have it my way, he'll be very lucky tonight.

Chapter Twenty One

Lynx

HOLY FUCK. SHE'S EVEN SEXIER in this outfit. I'm sure she's confused on how to dress because I told her we'd go to *Club Royal* tonight, but I've changed my mind. I want to take her somewhere where no one knows me and that isn't going to be *Club Royal*.

Hell, we both will be watched the entire night if we show up together and then it'll be even worse when we sit together all night. The way I am around her will be seen from clear across the fucking room. I just can't help it around her. She just makes me crazy.

"Are you ready?" She interrupts my thoughts as I stare at her.

"Yes. I'm taking you to a newer place downtown." She smiles. I can imagine she was thinking the same thing about the club.

We make our way outside and I straddle my bike. She looks at me as I get adjusted. "Have you ever done this before?" she asks me and I start laughing out loud.

"What part?" I hand her my helmet and move forward for her.

"Have you ever had a girl on the back?" I swallow hard. She doesn't want to know how many times I've done this.

"Yes, I've had someone on the back. Get on. I'll go slow since you look terrified." I let her get on and then pull her arms tighter around me. Before I take off, I rev up the engine and let it echo in the neighborhood. The sound of the rumble gets me excited to take her for a ride.

I may have lied when I told her I'd go slow. She holds on tight and I have to say I love how she feels with her arms around me.

We get to *Walker's Landing* and I park it up close to the front. This is a restaurant that's on the lake and I love to eat on the outside patio on nights like tonight. A nice dinner and some normal conversation is probably what she's after. I have to say I don't really care what we're doing. I just enjoy being around her.

"I thought you said you'd go slow?" she questions next to my ear.

Smiling, I help her down from my motorcycle and then get off myself. "I never go slow," I growl out. "And trying to when it comes to you is nearly fucking impossible. Let's go."

I slide my hand around her waist and guide her up the wooden dock that is lit up with white string lights. She looks around with a smile on her face as if me bringing her to a restaurant was the last thing she expected.

"This isn't a bar," she points out.

"It has one," I make clear. "Not that it needs to for me to bring you here."

The hostess flashes me a smile when she spots me walk in with my arm still slid securely around Rebel's waist. "Table for two?" she questions, while reaching for a couple of menus.

I nod my head. "A private table outside by the water."

"Excellent." She tries to sound enthused, but I can tell by the way her smile falters, that she's anything but. "Follow me."

Truthfully, *Walker's Landing* is a place that I like to come to alone to just relax and get my thoughts in check after a long week. This is the first time I have been accompanied by a woman and the hostess has tempted me many times here in the last couple months since they've been open.

The hostess takes us around the back to the private area and sets both of the menus down on the table, before stepping back and watching as I pull out a chair for Rebel to sit.

"Your waitress will be right with you."

I nod my head and take the seat across from Rebel as Melody walks away, mumbling under her breath.

She may be beautiful and tempting, but in all honesty, she doesn't even compare to Rebel. No one really does.

Rebel closes her eyes and smiles as a light breeze blows across her face. "This place is beautiful. It's the perfect night to eat out by the lake."

"I know," I respond. "It's something I do often."

We both look up as the waitress appears around the corner. An older woman in her late fifties.

"What a beautiful date night for young couples."

"It's not–" Rebel starts, but I quickly cut in.

"It is." I give Rebel a hard look and she blushes.

"My name is Mary and I'll be your server tonight. What can I start you out with to drink?"

My eyes land on Rebel, letting her know that I'm waiting on her to order first.

She hesitates for a moment. "Umm . . . how about a glass of white wine? Any one is fine."

"Make that a bottle," I add.

Mary nods. "And for you, Sir?"

"A water is fine."

"Sure." Mary smiles. "I'll be right back with your drinks and to take your orders."

"Maybe I should've just ordered soda." She flips through the menu, her eyes widening when she finds the price page for the wines. "I'm going to cancel that wine. You're only drinking water . . ."

She gets ready to walk away, but I grab her arm, stopping her. "Sit, Rebel."

"A bottle of white wine is over a hundred dollars. I don't need to drink wine, especially if you're only drinking water."

I grip her hips with both hands and pull her to me, in between my legs. I love feeling her so damn close to me. "I'm drinking water because there's no way in hell I'm going to put you on the back of my motorcycle even after one sip of alcohol. I'm buying and the wine is staying. Now take a seat and stop worrying."

Swallowing, she backs away from me and walks back over to sit in her seat. She's silent as she picks up the menu and begins looking through it.

I've been here enough to know exactly what I want before I even walk through the door.

Mary arrives a few minutes later with a bottle of white wine, shoved into a bucket of ice. She places the empty glass on the table, before setting my water in front of me and then pouring Rebel some wine.

"I'll take your orders if you're ready."

We give Mary our orders and thank her as she walks away.

"The service is here is fantastic. Very friendly." Rebel gives me a nervous smile and shifts in her seat as if she's not sure how to act. I'm sure she's wondering why I called this a date.

Because it fucking is.

"Come here," I command. I'm putting an end to this nervous bullshit right now. The last thing I want for her to feel is that I wouldn't take her on a fucking date. She's the first and probably only. "Now, Rebel," I push when she just looks at me.

Without a word, she stands up and walks over to stand in front of me. "Yeah?" she questions.

I pull her down into my lap and wrap both of my arms around her waist, holding her close against my chest. Having her in my lap feels so good and natural that it instantly gets my cock hard and my heart pumping fast.

She lets out a small moan as I press my lips just under her ear. "This *is* a date, Rebel. I wanted some alone time with you so stop sitting over there looking so confused about why we're here." My right hand moves up her body to wrap around the front of her neck, as I press my lips harder against her neck. "You have my head all fucked up with thoughts of you and you don't even have the slightest clue what you're doing to me. I like you, Rebel. I could give a shit that I'm your boss. I don't care for rules, much. Never have."

She moans out and grips my hand around her throat as I press my erection against her ass and grind. "Even the slightest thought of you keeps my dick hard," I breathe out. "No other woman has control over my dick or my mind. Only you."

Her free hand runs over my thigh, before she squeezes it and digs her nails in. "Stop grinding against me like that. I can't handle that shit right now."

"Why?" I question, while grinding my hips again and squeezing her throat tighter. "Because you want me just as much as I fucking want you and you can't control it. Just like me. You don't truly care that I'm your boss. Admit it."

Rebels just about to speak, when Mary clears her throat

from behind us. "Your food is ready."

Fuck me . . .

Rebel pulls my hand away from her throat and quickly jumps from my lap, making her way back over to her seat. "Thank you," she says as Mary sets her plate down in front of her.

I keep my eyes on Rebel as she digs into her food. My words have worked her up and I love it. There's no hiding just how much she truly wants me.

I thank Mary and nod as she disappears, leaving us alone again.

We don't speak again until we're half way through our meals.

"Do you enjoy graphic design?" I ask out of curiosity, wanting to get to know her outside of her life at the Alpha House.

She nods her head. "I do, but being on the computer too much hurts my eyes. I think I may even have to get contacts soon."

"Does it hurt your eyes when you're at the office working?"

"No." She takes a bite of her pork and quickly chews and swallows, before speaking again. "Being on the computer isn't constant when I'm working at the office. It gives me time to rest my eyes."

"Good." I finish off my plate and push it aside. "If you ever need time away from the computer, let me know and I'll think of a few other things for you to do."

"I'm good." She smiles, appreciatively. "Thank you for that."

"The last thing I want is for you to be uncomfortable."

She lets out an amused laugh. "Really? Is that why you're always pushing me sexually?"

I flex my jaw and answer her honestly. "No. That's because I can't stop myself from wanting you every second of the fucking day."

"Are you always like that with your female employees?" She takes her last bite and challenges me with her eyes. She wants to know for her own reasons and the look in her eyes tells me that she's hoping I say no.

"Never," I say sternly. "I always keep it professional with my employees. You're the exception."

She sips her wine and runs her tongue over her lips, licking off the excess wine. It's now her third glass since arriving and she's beginning to get bolder with each sip. "What about the girls that call you? I bet you've fucked a few of them."

My jaw ticks. She really has no clue that with each word that leaves her mouth, I only want to bend her over this dock and fuck her even more. "I have."

"How many?" she questions.

"A few." Keep going. *Go ahead.*

"Do you really want to talk about our pasts?" She sits up straight before she responds to my question.

"Alright I'll go first. I had a boyfriend that fucked around on me and I'm not about to go in that direction again." Her serious face saddens me. I wish I could beat a fucker's ass, but honestly I should thank him. He didn't have the morals to keep her, I won't make the same mistake. "What about you?"

"I've been around the block a few times, but never anything real serious. I guess you could say not many women can handle my intensity." Her eyes light up as she watches me rub my beard to hide the smile on my face.

"You've never had a serious relationship?"

"Nope. I've never really met anyone I liked well enough to keep them around for long."

We stop as Mary grabs our plates and brings us the bill.

"We're going to need a while," I say, while keeping my eyes on Rebel and tossing Mary a hundred-dollar tip. "At least an hour."

Mary's eyes widen, but she grabs the money and smiles. "Yes, Sir. Take your time."

"What was that about?" Rebel asks, looking confused. "We're done eating."

"I'm not." Standing from my seat, I pull Rebel to her feet and back her up against the wooden railing. Without hesitation, I grip her jeans and yank them down her legs. "This is exactly why I asked for no panties."

"What are you . . . right here . . ."

Her lips stop moving, the second my mouth crashes against her warm, wet pussy and over her throbbing clit.

My tongue works slowly at first to spread the moisture up her folds, before I take her clit into my mouth and gently suck it, growling against her pussy.

This is mine and I'm claiming it right now, making sure she knows how much I love it.

She moans out from the vibration of my mouth and grips my hair so hard that it makes my cock jump.

After a few seconds of her squirming above me, I release her clit and bring my tongue down further, shoving it into her pussy as deep as it will go, fucking her nice and slow with my tongue, allowing myself to taste her without rushing.

"Fuck," I groan against her pussy. "I love the taste of you on my tongue, Rebel. So fucking good."

"Oh shit . . ." she moans, while gripping my hair even harder. "I can't believe . . ."

Her words fade out as I run the tip of my tongue between her folds and then suck her clit into my mouth again, but harder this time, while holding her leg above my head for better access.

I dig my fingers into her thigh and swirl my tongue around her now swollen clit, before shoving my tongue back into her aching pussy and fucking her with my tongue again.

"Keep going . . . keep . . . oh God. I'm about to . . ." her fingers tangle and pull at my hair with desperation as she shakes under my grip and moans out her pleasure.

There's no doubt in my mind that everyone around the corner of the dock just heard her get off to my tongue fucking her tight little pussy. That only turns me on more, making me almost desperate to be inside her. Only, I need more privacy for this, because she's going to scream louder than she ever has before.

"Let's get out of here so I can do what I really want to you."

I just hope she can handle how much I want her right now . . .

Chapter Twenty Two

Rebel

I HAVE NO IDEA WHAT JUST happened back there at the restaurant, but I can't deny that I loved it more than I should've.

Him pleasuring me with his tongue in a public place, with no worries about who might just catch us. Talk about a fucking rush. I've never experienced a high like it in my life. Not even close.

My grip on him with my right arm tightens as he takes my left hand and shoves it down the front of his body and down to his erect dick.

I become oblivious to being on the back of a moving motorcycle and everything else around me, and all I can think about is just how sexy this is right now.

His thickness feels so good under my hand and before I know it, his jeans are unzipped and he's slowing down to free his dick from his boxer briefs.

It's completely dark outside, but the lights from the side streets will give away what we're doing if anyone attempts to pull up next to us and watch.

He doesn't seem to care . . . so neither do I.

Being careful to hold on tightly with my right arm, I grip his shaft with my left hand and slowly begin stroking his length.

He leans his head back and growls under his breath as I run my finger over the pre-cum beading at the head of his dick.

"Oh fuck!" He speeds up a little as if he's in a hurry to get me back to his place, but then stops as the light ahead turns red. Growling, he grips my hand that's on his dick, making me grab it harder. "Keep stroking me like that and I'm going to come all over this fucking motorcycle."

"That's my plan," I say teasingly, while gently running my thumb over his new piercing. "I'm not stopping until you do."

The light turns green. "Fuck!" he shouts, while taking off and gripping the handles so hard that his knuckles turn white.

He's so damn thick and hard, that it's nearly impossible to stroke him with only one hand, but I'm not letting go of him and risking my life. This may be hot, but not *that* hot. So I do my best with what I have available to me.

When the Alpha Mansion comes into view, Lynx stops at the end of the driveway and grips my hand aiming his dick to the right, squeezing it as his hot cum shoots out onto the gravel, next to his boots.

"Oh fuck!" He breathes heavily, while still holding my hand on his dick. "I can't handle that shit. What the fuck am I going to do with you, Rebel?"

Wanting to push him just as he's pushed me, I lean up and speak next to his ear. "Take me inside and fuck me hard. Don't hold back. I want to scream so loud that the whole house hears."

"That's my plan," he grinds out, while pulling up to the gate and letting us in since the guard is off tonight.

He barely parks the motorcycle before grabbing my arm and

yanking me off, then he jumps off himself and pulls me against him.

His hand is quick to undo my jeans and pull them down enough to slide his finger up my wet slit.

"Oh shit!" Someone screams from by the pool. "Take her pants off!"

"Fuck off, Rome! Close your eyes and go the fuck inside. Now."

"Not a chance," Blaze says, now joining Rome by the water. "Don't start shit in front of us that you're not going to finish."

Lynx leans his head down into my neck and growls out his frustration.

"Fuckers, you will never watch her do a damn thing." He stands between me and the guys and holds me close to his body. "Now go the fuck inside or I'll evict your asses in the morning. I'm not kidding."

I hear laughter coming from the pool and now realize there's more than just the two of them out there. I can hardly comprehend what's being said because Lynx hasn't let up on me, in fact he's increased the pressure as he circles my clit over and over before sliding his finger inside me.

"We need a camera in the pool area. I'll bring that shit up at the next meeting!" one of the guys yells from the door and I can feel the frustration building in Lynx as he continues to hold me close, never pulling his hand from between my legs.

"Get. The. Motherfuck. Out of here. Before I kill you." He turns just slightly, never leaving me exposed.

"It's all yours, Boss."

He slows his movements against me and I can see the smile spread across his face just as he hears the door slide closed.

"She sure is." His lips cover mine and I step in closer as he wraps me up into his arms. He smells so good and I find myself practically on my tip toes as he continues to provide the best type of friction where I crave it most.

"I want you naked." His deep voice in my ear sounds as desperate as I feel.

"They'll come out."

"No they won't." He pulls my bottom lip between his teeth before he slides his hand between us, placing his fingers in his mouth, tasting me once again. "Fuck, you're going to be the death of me, Rebel. I'm already hard even after the stunt you pulled back there."

I love that he has stamina and can bounce back this quick. It seems my appetite for sex is much larger when I'm near him than it has ever been before. He's changing me and I'm beginning to like the way he makes me feel.

"Step out of these." He tugs on my jeans and stands to watch me. I look around and see the front of the house and decide to move us to the back where the pool is. At least if someone comes out, I have a chance to hide in the water if I have to.

I take his hand and lead him to a lounge chair before I give him a little shove so he'll sit down.

"Don't move." I know how he loves to play games and I think it's only right that I keep up with his tactics. What can I say? He just brings this out in me.

He watches me with a very large smile on his face, probably anticipating what I'm about to do. He likes surprises just like I do, so I know he'll like what he's about to see.

I turn away from him and slowly slide my jeans down my body, bending at the waist, making sure he sees my ass in the moonlight.

"I'm gonna fuck that ass if you keep this up." His words bring a smile to my face because I know this show will be torture for him.

"No one's been there before," I say in a low growl. "I'm not so sure I'd let you."

I kick my jeans aside and look behind me to see him palming his dick through his jeans as he watches me with hooded eyes. "You would and you will. Keep going."

Stepping closer to him, I pull my bottom lip between my teeth and grab the bottom of my shirt, slowly pulling it up my body and over my head. I can tell by the way his eyes are watching me with desperation that he's dying to pull me onto his lap and onto his waiting dick.

I asked him to make me scream and now he wants to more than ever just to show me how loud he can.

"Lose the bra," he bites out. "Then come and stand between my legs."

Smirking, I undo my bra and let it fall down the front of my body. Then I take a few teasing steps, until I'm right between his opened legs and tangling my hands into the back of his thick hair.

"Fuck me, you've definitely fucked my world up and you're not leaving here until I've returned the favor."

Gripping my hip with one hand, he shoves the other one into his pocket and reaches for a condom, pulling it out and biting it open with his teeth.

It's so sexy the way his teeth dig into the wrapper with a need that he can't seem to control and I find myself getting impatient myself.

My body shivers with excitement as he lowers his jeans just enough to free his erection and slides the condom on, working his hand over his length a few times.

Looking up at me, he reaches up with both hands and grips the back of my hair, pulling me down onto his cock so that I'm straddling him. Growling out in pleasure, he pulls me down, slowly sliding inside of me, inch by inch, until I'm completely filled by him.

He feels so damn good and there's no denying that I've been going crazy to feel him inside of me again.

Growling, he tangles his hands deeper into the back of my hair to the scalp and thrusts his hips into me, hard. So hard that I bounce up from his lap and fall back down, my breath getting knocked out of me. The way his dick slams back into my pussy has me gasping and holding onto him as tightly as I can, biting my lip from the intense pain.

I let out a loud moan when he begins moving again after a few seconds of letting me adjust, loving the way he feels so deep inside of me. He's so thick and long, taking care of every single need, unlike anyone else has been able to.

Pushing me down against him as roughly as he can, he thrusts his hips a few times, grinding his erection inside of my now aching pussy, while brushing his lips against my ear and gently kissing me.

His rhythm has me almost dying above him, and I can tell by the satisfied look in his eyes and his devilish grin that he knows he has me right where he wants me and there's no way I won't be leaving here with my world completely fucked like his.

Whatever he meant by that . . .

He yanks my head back with force and bites my neck, while pushing into me as deep as he possibly can and stilling. His tongue works my neck, easing the pain from his bite, as he pulls out and thrusts back into me, even harder as if it's just not enough. "I love your pussy, Rebel. I don't plan on fucking sharing."

Tilting my head back, he runs his tongue over my mouth, before sucking my lip into his mouth as he rolls his hips, making me moan into his mouth.

He pulls away from the kiss and licks his lips as if to taste me on them. He's so rough and unfiltered and I love it. It's a complete turn on and so different from anything I've experienced. He makes me want so much more than what I'm used to. I want it and with him.

Pounding into me hard, he grabs my throat and pushes my neck back, tightening his grip as we get lost in each other. He's holding it so tightly that I can barely breathe for a minute, until his grip loosens and he leans in to press a soft kiss against my lips.

I scream out in a mixture of pleasure and pain when he pulls away, only causing him to go faster and harder. I don't want him to stop being rough. I want to feel what's inside this man. I want all of Lynx and even the thought of him being inside of another woman like this has me going completely crazy inside.

"Keep screaming and I'm only going to fuck you harder and make you scream louder."

I pull his hair and slam myself down hard onto his dick, surprising him. "Good," I whisper against his ear. "Let the others know that I'm yours." My face instantly heats up, surprised at myself for what just came out of my mouth.

I'm his?

He must be surprised too, because his rhythm slows as if letting the words sink in. Then without warning, he pulls my face to his and slams his lips hard against mine, as his speed picks back up, him taking me hard and deep again.

His lips devour mine with such eagerness that his teeth get my bottom lip, drawing blood. Placing his forehead to mine, he sucks my bottom lip into his mouth with a gentleness that melts my damn heart. "Fuck. I'm sorry, baby."

I shake my head and rub my fingers over his lips, my heart racing from him calling me baby. "Don't be."

Holding onto me tightly, he picks me up and kicks his jeans off before he walks us over to the waterfall. Standing under the water, he kisses me long and deep, while gently lifting me up and down as he thrusts into me.

The warm water slides down our bodies and we both just close our eyes and move with each other. It's such a special moment and I know I'll never look at this waterfall the same again.

The way he holds me and touches my entire body with his literally melts me. It's almost like I can see a softness in his eyes as he continues to move in and out of me as we both hide behind the water fall.

He takes me closer to my release with each thrust of his hips and the whole time his dark brown eyes continue to stare deep into mine.

He's deep. In more ways than one.

Digging my fingernails into his back, I roll through another epic orgasm from him only to have him follow right behind me, holding onto me for dear life.

"You fucking make me crazy. I've never wanted to literally fuck someone every single time I'm with them." I'm still breathing deeply as I try to respond to his way of being sincere.

"I know what you mean."

"Stay the night with me." He surprises me with his request.

How the hell do I tell him no, because that's exactly what I have to do?

Chapter Twenty Three

Lynx

HOW THE FUCK HAVE I let this get as far as it has? I just asked her to stay the night with me. My dick is betraying me in every way with her.

I told her I don't have rules, but the truth is, I have one. *Kick them out after sex.*

And here I've invited her to stay the night. *What the fuck is wrong with me?*

"I can't." The second she says no, I'm irritated. I should be relieved, but no. My fucked up mind is frustrated that she's again pulling away from me. She slides down from around my hips, but we both stay behind the water, breathing heavily.

"You're really going to fuck and run?" I mean, that's the kind of shit I would do. I'm just not used to a woman being adamant about it. From her, it has my chest aching.

"It's really not a good idea for me to stay. If I do, then you'll expect it all the time."

"So the fuck what. I mean, we already know the sex would

be great if you stayed in my bed." She's looking down as I talk to her. I can practically feel her trying to decide how to leave, so I do something that even surprises me.

I dip down and lift her onto my shoulder. She screams at me when I start to walk toward the back door of my house. We're both dripping wet and completely naked. This is going to suck, but it's the statement I'm willing to make.

"You'd better cover yourself." I don't even bother trying to cover my dick, in fact I slide the condom off and hold it in one hand while the other one holds her ass in place on my shoulder.

Opening the door in a hurry, I storm past the guys in the kitchen, drop the condom in the trash while surprisingly none of them say a word the entire time she's cussing at me.

"What the hell, Lynx. I swear I'm going to get you back for this shit." Her arms are no longer beating against my ass, so I can only assume she's covering those gorgeous tits.

"I can't wait to see you try, baby. It will bring a smile to my fucking face." I keep walking up the stairs and down the hall until I can set her down in my bedroom.

She looks roughed up and soaking wet when she looks up at me. I can't help but laugh at her when she hits my arm with her fist.

"What the fuck is wrong with you? You live in a house full of men and you just walked us both through the house completely naked."

"You're going to stay the night and spend time with me tonight. Unless you want to walk back through the house to get your clothes that you dropped out by the pool."

"You ass. If you wanted me to stay, you should've just said it." I think about her response. Hell, I didn't even know I wanted her to stay this much and I sure as shit didn't plan to parade her through the house.

"I told you to stay. And besides that, this can give us more time to talk tonight. That is if I can concentrate with you standing naked in my bedroom."

She looks even more irritated now. "Can I at least borrow a t-shirt?" Now she's walking to my closet without even waiting for my response. She pulls out a plain white t-shirt and slips it over her head.

I grab a pair of my shorts from the dresser and slide them up my legs before I sit on the couch to watch her pace.

"Did you really just take me through the Alpha House over your damn shoulder like a barbarian? I mean shit, Lynx, I was naked."

"I promise they didn't see anything unless you didn't cover your tits." She stops to glare at me for a second.

"Yes I tried to cover them, but it's not easy you know with these." She points to her tits, reminding me just how large they really are. "Especially when I'm hanging upside down like some rag doll." She finally sits next to me and pulls the t-shirt down lower to cover herself.

"It's all good. I think they were all too shocked to say anything." I'm really surprised Blaze didn't. He must not have been in the kitchen, because he would've hands down made sure to yell something obscene at us.

She takes a deep breath and looks at me. Her eyes move over my face fully before she busts out laughing. "You're insane! I can't believe you just hauled me naked through the house just to get your way." I pull her so that she's laying with her head across my lap as she continues to laugh.

"Yeah, I kind of surprised myself on that move. But I'm used to getting what I want, so just remember that." She looks up at me while I run my fingers through her long brown hair.

"I can see that! But next time just tell me again, or give

me some sort of code." I nod at her and smile. "I figured the guys would be working tonight." She adjusts herself a little lower on the couch after she changes the subject. I notice her nipples through the shirt, so I run my finger over them slowly as I answer.

"We've scheduled a few off nights each week. I know it'll suck for scheduling, but it'll keep the guys from getting burnt out. This shit gets monotonous after a while and most of my guys have been doing it since the beginning."

"That's probably good for them anyway. They need to have somewhat of a life outside the computer screen." She turns to her side and pulls my arm into her chest like she's cuddling it. The t-shirt slides up her back and she doesn't move to cover her ass again. I notice it, but don't move from her hold to run my hand over it like I normally would.

"They do." She lays quietly for a while and I can feel her wheels turning about the business. I've learned that women don't usually love what I do once they've made it to this level. In all actuality women don't make it to this point, but they tend to get jealous when the business comes into it.

"Are you into BDSM?" I look at the cross and smile at her question.

"I've never really done too much with the actual BDSM furniture, but as you can tell by my sexual appetite, I'd be into most any sexual activity with a woman. Besides, I think I have a slightly dominant personality."

"Slightly?" She laughs out loud and sits up while her eyes never leave the cross.

"I've always been curious about one of these." She moves from the couch to walk around it, allowing her fingers to slide over the straps as she does.

I watch with a smile on my face, knowing how good this

will be.

"Take your shirt off and I'll show you how it works." She looks over at me, surprised by my words as I stand to move with her.

"I think it's only fair we make a night of it soon. We can take turns on it." I flinch at the thought of being tied up by a woman before I look at her. She's still staring at all the straps trying to wrap her own head around it.

"I look forward to it."

"Me too. I'll think about all the ways I can tease you." Her eyes meet mine as she begins to toss around ideas in her head.

"Come here." I decide not to wait on this little game. This will be more fun if we just go with what we're feeling instead of planning a bunch of shit to do to each other.

She moves toward me with a small smile on her face. She knows what's coming. "Shirt off. Now." I watch her slowly lift it over her body, uncovering everything that haunts my life lately.

I send goose bumps over her when I let my finger slide over her daisy tattoo before I grab her wrists tightly in both of my hands.

"You're going to listen to everything I say." She swallows hard before she looks down at my hands holding hers. Pulling away from my grip, she steps closer to the cross giving me an expression that invites me to bring whatever I want to the table.

Her hair is still wet, yet she looks the sexiest I've seen her look right here in this very moment. She's letting me control her and there's something appealing about a woman who's willing to do that.

"Put your legs against the wood." She lines her legs up with the cross and I lean over to strap her ankles then upper legs to the cross. This cross is adjustable, so I spread her legs even further apart with a simple movement of a latch.

She raises her arms as I work my way up her body. Fuck, she's sexy as hell and damn it if my dick isn't *already* twitching again.

"I'm going to blindfold you." I don't want her to know where I'm at. After walking to the closet to pick out a tie, I quickly cover her eyes and stand back to take her in.

There's a smile on her face even though she's pulling her bottom lip in with her teeth.

"You're sexy as fuck, Rebel." Her nipples are hard and her muscles are all pulled tight as she's held in place by all the straps. I could just look at her like this forever.

I move a chair to sit directly in front of her and watch the way her body reacts to every sound in the room. A knock at the door has her breathing heavy before I even have the chance to acknowledge it.

"What do you want?"

"We're headed out to *Club Royal*. You'll have the house to yourself unless you want to go with us." Blaze opens the door to talk to me and the smirk on his face both frustrates me and makes me proud. He sees how sexy she is just like this and he knows she's off limits.

"No, I'm good here. Text me before you guys head back." This makes me happy. I need some damn privacy and I couldn't have asked for a more perfect night for that to happen.

"Will do. Have fun." I don't respond to him. My eyes haven't left her body as I watch her react to the sound of him in the room. The change in her body is deafening. She likes to be watched.

"Wait, Blaze." I stop him from leaving, but signal for him to look away. He follows my lead perfectly before I turn to tease Rebel.

"You like the thought of him watching you like this, don't

you?" She begins to shake her head no instantly, obviously trying to deny what her body is screaming as I watch her.

"I can tell by the way your body is responding that you're turned on by him seeing you like this." She stands still with no response.

"You want him to fuck you too?" That gets an immediate no from her.

"You want him to touch you?" She instantly stops moving.

Holy shit, this girl is a fucking freak and I love it, but there's no fucking way she's going to feel his touch.

Rebel

OH SHIT . . . *that's a surprise.*

I never really thought about someone else watching or touching me until Lynx brought it to my attention. Now my whole body is heated at just the thought of Blaze's eyes on me, watching whatever it is that Lynx plans to do to me. Or possibly even touching me. *Can I handle his touch?*

I'd love to see if this new sexual desire I seem to have is solely for Lynx or if I'm changing into some sex craved maniac. Right now I'm not sure if it's the heat from Lynx's stare that has me going or the fact that I'm crossing into uncharted territory having two men watch me at once.

I'm guessing it's the anticipation of what Lynx will do in this situation. It's one way to see how he feels about me. If he wants me like I want him, he won't want to share. I guess this is the best way to prove that to him. The air changes as I hear someone move closer. I can barely breathe waiting for something to happen.

My heart is beating out of control as I try to still my mind from the chaos of everything going on. This is all so hot, dark and twisted and I'm not sure if I can handle all of this.

"I don't know if I want him to touch me . . . no," I attempt to convince Lynx, but truthfully, my words aren't even enough to convince myself. Being cuffed here, useless and blindfolded has my body wanting things I never even imagined.

"Don't be ashamed. Fucking own what your body wants, Rebel." I hear him stand up from his chair and then feel the heat from his body as he comes to stand in front of me. "You want his eyes on you as I touch you like this?"

My back arches and a small moan escapes my lips when I feel him take my right nipple between his teeth and gently play with it, biting it. The sensation is unlike anything I've ever felt before.

The mystery and anticipation of what he's going to do next has my body completely lashing out, dying to find out where his mouth or hands will end up.

My whole body is covered in goose bumps, yet I'm completely fucking hot and sweaty.

His tongue darts out and swirls slow circles around my nipple, as he pulls the latch, spreading my legs apart even more, leaving me completely vulnerable to him.

He has the power to touch me, kiss me and taste me anywhere he wants and I'm completely fucking powerless. He could even let Blaze do all those things and truth be known, I couldn't do anything to stop them, but I know Lynx wouldn't hurt me. If I said stop, he would in a second.

"Lynx," I moan out. "Touch me. Please," I beg.

His teeth tug my nipple as he growls out his satisfaction and need to be in control. He's completely silent after that and I feel as if I'm going to go crazy, while my body waits for his touch.

My whole body jerks and need runs throughout my entire body, heating me to my core, when I feel his warm breath blow against my aching pussy. His mouth is so close, yet not close enough and I can't handle it. I want to scream so damn bad and rip at his hair, but my hands are bound above me.

"Fuck, Rebel. Look at you." I feel the tip of his stiff tongue, gently run up my slit, teasing me. "Your body is so ready for me, Rebel." He runs his tongue between my folds, before capturing my swollen clit in his mouth and nibbling it. "So damn wet."

"Oh fuck!" I scream through heavy breaths, while thrusting my hips closer to his mouth with desperation. "I can't handle it, Lynx. Not tonight," I pant. "Please . . ."

"If I give you what you want . . ." He flicks his tongue out again, making my entire body shake with pleasure. "Will you let me tie you up again?" He moves his face from side to side, letting his facial hair rub over my sensitive clit.

"Yes!" I scream out. "Yes. I'll do anything."

With that, his mouth crashes against my pussy, licking and sucking on every aching part of it, making me scream out as I come against his hot mouth.

My body trembles from the rush of emotions flowing through me while he takes in every single bit of my orgasm with his tongue.

"Oh shit, Lynx," I breathe once my body starts to come down from its high. "Get me down from here."

I hear the door open and close and the realization that Blaze just left without touching me both relieves me and disappoints me. *What in the hell is wrong with me?*

Leaving the blindfold in place, Lynx works to undo my arms, before moving down to my feet and freeing them and taking me into his arms.

"I wanted to do more to you," he says, his voice, deep and

full of need. "Next time I won't be so easy on you."

My body relaxes as he gently lays me in the bed and scoots in behind me, pressing his body against mine. He trails kisses over my body, while rubbing me with his fingers as if he can't get enough of touching me. It's as if he wants to remember every last inch of me.

His touch is gentle and I can't deny that it has my heart completely open to him. I never imagined I'd be with Lynx this way, but I seriously want it more now than ever.

The craziness that happens when I'm with him is addicting and I'm not sure I'm ready to go back to the boring life I led before I met him.

My test for him didn't really answer anything. I can't tell if he kept Blaze from touching me or if he just didn't want any part of me. Now that I'm lying here in Lynx's arms, I'm really glad Blaze didn't do more than he did. It was a line that we didn't need to cross.

I'm not sure if what happened was a good or bad thing. All I know is my heart is aching for something I might not be able to fully have.

Chapter Twenty Four

Rebel

I WAKE UP THE NEXT morning to a note left in his place and a tray full of food with a lid, keeping it warm.

Eat and then come down to work when you're ready.

I can't help the smile that takes over as I toss the note aside and open the tray to see pancakes, bacon, sausage, eggs and hash browns. It looks completely delicious.

It's been a long time since I've had a home cooked meal before work. I usually just run down the street and grab a bagel or some takeout before I start my day. This is a treat that I could definitely get used to.

I'm halfway through my meal when I hear vibrating coming from close by. Sitting up on my knees, I catch my phone about to fall off the dresser.

Hurrying to my feet, I rush to my phone, realizing that I was so exhausted last night that I forgot to tell Remi that I wouldn't be coming home.

"Don't flip out," I say as soon as I accept the call. "Shit . . . I'm sorry I didn't call you–"

"What the hell, Rebel! You're lucky that I knew you were safe in the hands of the damn sexist man on the Internet. I almost showed up outside the damn gate and climbed over it."

I laugh into the phone. "That would've been for your benefit, not mine. Although, with security you wouldn't have made it far."

"Yeah . . ." she sounds like she's brushing her teeth. She spits into the sink. "It's part of being desperate. Have you met Rome yet? I have a call with him next week. I booked last night. And Blaze. Oh my god. I saw on the website that he has a fucking twin. A twin! You know I've always fantasized about two hot twins."

I roll my eyes and pop the last piece of bacon in my mouth, quickly chewing as I talk. "I've seen Rome. He's cute . . . and so is Blaze."

"Cute?" She laughs into my ear. "Correction. Hot as fuck."

"I'd love to spend the morning talking to you about the boys, but I need to be in the office in thirty minutes. I need a quick shower before I start the day."

"I bet you do. Did Lynx dirty you up last night with his fine body? Did he tie you up and take you hard? He looks like that kind of man."

I shake my head and run my hand over my face. "Gotta go, Remi. I'll see you tonight."

Before she gets the chance to speak again, I hit end on the call and toss my cell down beside me. Looking around the room, I see that my clothes from last night are neatly folded on top of the dresser, next to where my phone was.

I was in such a hurry to grab my phone, that I didn't even notice them stacked up. Walking over to the dresser, I pick up my shirt and sniff. Someone washed my clothes for me. I'm guessing Lynx, which makes me wonder what time he gets up in the morning.

Hopping into the shower, I quickly clean up, my mind stuck on Lynx the entire fifteen minutes that the warm water hits against my skin. It reminds me of the waterfall last night and my body instantly heats up at the thought of him touching me.

Knowing that I'll be seeing him soon has my heart racing with an excitement that I don't feel too often.

"Shit, that's not good," I say to myself, while throwing my hair up and taking a quick glance in the mirror, while throwing on some lip gloss. "This will have to do."

Grabbing my purse, I make my way through the quiet house. It seems most of the guys don't wake up until around ten or at least don't come out of their rooms until then. So there's no one in sight as I let myself into the office and close the door behind me.

I immediately turn on the computer and get to work, setting up schedules for the next four weeks and taking payments for the calls happening tomorrow night.

My heart starts to beat faster as I scroll down the waiting list for Lynx, seeing at least a hundred names, trying to get scheduled in for the first available appointments.

A part of me almost wants to delete them all and I hate myself for that thought ever even occurring. I have no business worrying about how many girls are waiting to watch him get naked for them.

"Morning." I look up at the sound of Lynx's deep voice. "Did you sleep well last night?"

Clearing my throat, I smile and force the thought of him

showing that insanely hot body off to the hundreds of women that are waiting impatiently to get their turn. "Yes, thank you." I watch as he walks into the office and stops to stand in front of me. "Thanks for breakfast." I point down at my clothes. "And for washing my clothes."

"Come here." He grabs my hand and pulls me up to my feet. His dark eyes scan my face, before he wraps his hands into the back of my hair and presses his lips against mine, kissing me slow and hot.

My body instantly reacts to his, my hands coming up to wrap around his neck. It feels so damn natural that it's scary. "I'm guessing you found the guest toothbrush I left you?" he questions, while running his tongue over his bottom lip.

I nod my head and close my eyes as his thumb caresses my bottom lip. "Good. I'll keep it in my bathroom for when you stay with me."

"Stay with you?" I question, my heart hammering in my chest.

"I didn't stutter, Rebel. You will be spending nights here with me. I want you close to me." His warm breath covers my ear, before he sucks my earlobe into his mouth and speaks again. "I loved waking up to you in my bed. I could get used to it."

"I thought it was a onetime thing," I admit. "In the heat of the moment."

His hands slowly run down my back, before stopping to cup my ass. "Nothing is ever a onetime thing with you, Rebel. There might be a lot of things that happen in the heat of the moment, but they're things that I want to happen."

He grips my ass and sucks my bottom lip into his mouth, before releasing it and smirking. "You'll most likely be busy in the office all day, so I'll make sure the guys stay away and let you work."

I stand here completely silent, at a loss for words as he walks out of the office, closing the door behind him.

He wants me to stay with him?

Nothing is a onetime thing with me?

He acted like nothing awkward or out of line happened last night. I get an unsettled feeling that this relationship isn't going to last long if I can't get a grip on the reality of the way things are with him. He's obviously not ever going to be a normal relationship. If I decide to continue with him, I need to prepare myself for the insanity he will bring into my life and decide if I'm emotionally strong enough to deal with someone like him.

Sitting back down at the desk, I stare at the computer screen, my eyes becoming blurry as I take in all of the profile names.

The more time I spend with Lynx, the more I'm going to hate scheduling these women to watch him take his clothes off and touch himself for them.

Is this something that I can really get mixed up in? Can I spend time with Lynx and not fall for him? Can I really handle women getting off to him?

Every single answer leads to no. No fucking way.

Knowing that I need to keep it professional, while I'm at work, I begin scheduling Lynx's calls. He has twenty-eight set up for next week alone. That's four calls a day: four women getting off to him within twenty-four damn hours.

Gritting my teeth, I move onto taking his payments for his scheduled appointments for tomorrow. Who the hell makes over five grand a day just for taking off their clothes? The Alpha men, apparently. Hell, that means most of them can make up to twenty-five grand a week or more.

"This is insane," I whisper to myself. "Just fucking insane."

By the time I get done for the day, all I want to do is go home and bury my head in my pillow. My thoughts have been screwing with me all day and stressing me out. Now, I know what Lynx meant by not letting me leave here until my world is fucked up by him.

Last night definitely got under my skin, making it completely impossible to shove him from my mind.

Letting myself out of the office, I shut it behind me and take off down the hall, not sure if I can look at Lynx's face right now or hear the deepness of his sexy voice.

I just need to get away to the comfort of my own home, where I can think clearly.

When I make it to the stairs, I look over the railing to see the guys all gathered up, in the living room. It looks like some kind of group meeting and Lynx is caught up in talking.

Shit!

I freeze, hoping not to draw attention my way, but every single set of eyes are suddenly locked on me, making me instantly break out in a sweat.

How the hell am I supposed to survive being in the same room as ten of the most gorgeous and sexual men in the world?

"Rebel." Lynx speaks up, as some of the guys begin whistling up at me. "Come here." He turns to Blaze and says something, but I don't catch it.

Blaze runs his hand over the front of his sweats. "How the fuck am I not supposed to have a boner after seeing her last night?"

My face heats up in embarrassment at the realization that he saw me completely naked and moaning through an orgasm and at least four of Lynx's other guys have seen my tits. I did my best to cover them up, but my arms could only cover so much.

"You will or I'll fuck your ass up so hard that your twin will feel my wrath," he growls out. He turns to Rome. "You too."

Rome grabs a pillow and shoves it over his crotch. "Shit. My bad."

Pushing everything to the back of my mind, I walk over to stand next to Lynx. I suck in a surprised breath as he grabs my hip and pulls me next to him, possessively.

"No one touches Rebel. No one jerks off to Rebel. When you know she's here, you will give a fucking warning before you decide to jerk off anywhere that isn't in your damn room or the privacy of the gym. Got it?"

"Got it," the guys take turns agreeing. I don't know what all of his threats mean after last night. This is definitely something we need to talk about.

"We have another party to set up for tomorrow night for our clients and we need to come up with a theme. Most of you have already sent out your invitations. Think on what you want and drop me your ideas later so we can get the emails sent out tonight."

The guys sound their excitement as they all scatter around the house, most likely ready to start their day. I know for a fact that Nash has a call in less than thirty minutes. Most of the others don't have any until tonight.

He's the only one that rushes off to his room to most likely prepare.

As soon as the room clears out, Lynx cups my face and turns his body to face me. "Where are you going?" he asks against my lips.

I place both of my hands on his arms. "I'm headed home to relax and get some more work in later."

His eyes study me as if he can tell I'm stressing about something. "You want to talk about it?"

I can't just tell him how I feel about him taking calls from other women after the way I acted last night. It's not like we're dating. What right do I have?

"There's nothing to talk about. I think I just need a nap in my own bed."

He runs his thumb down my cheek, before leaning in to press his lips against mine. "Message me when you have free time. I have some shit to take care of around here before my calls for tonight. Want me to drop you off?"

My stomach twists up into knots and my heart sinks, letting me know that this isn't going to be easy to get past.

I shake my head and smile. "Remi's outside. I'm fine. I'll message you when I get time."

With that, I walk away from him, letting myself outside, thinking hard about what I need to do next.

The problem is . . . I have no idea what he even wants from me and I'm scared to find out.

Chapter Twenty Five

Lynx

I WAITED ALL NIGHT TO hear from Rebel, but she never messaged me. Hell, I even kept my phone close by while taking every single one of my calls last night, just so I could see if I missed a text from her.

Not a damn thing.

I almost showed up at her doorstep last night and punished her with my cock to remind her just how much I want her and how much she fucks with my head.

Instead, I sat at her office desk and looked over all of the work that she did for the day. When I sat down at the desk and woke the computer back up, the screen with my waiting list was sitting there, staring back at me.

Fuck . . . no wonder she didn't message me last night. After the night she shared in my bed, I'm sure the last thing she wanted to see was the list of all of the women that I'll be jerking my shit for over the next few weeks.

If it were the other way I around, I'd look up every one of

those fucker's addresses and end up at their doorstep, ready to fuck them up and break the hand they get off with.

Tonight is another Alpha party and I want Rebel to be here, but I have a feeling that she might not want to now. Especially since I had Blaze watch her last night. I could tell it's something she wanted to do and fuck if she wasn't completely turned on knowing he was watching. I'm trying to decide how I feel about that. I know Blaze would never cross any boundaries I don't lay out. The only thing I knew was that I wasn't ready to see his hands on her. It was bad enough that his eyes were watching her come undone.

I had Blaze send out a random invite to ten of my girls. I could give two fucks about who he chose. I won't be spending any time with them.

The parties are to help the other guys get new clients. The only woman I plan to spend my time with is Rebel, so I need her here tonight.

We've decided on a black tie affair. I had Rome pick up some bow ties and skimpy ass underwear for all of us to wear. The women will all be in evening gowns, but I'm sure they'll all be unique in revealing themselves.

I send a text to Rebel again and she still doesn't respond. Her silence is fucking with my mind because I don't know if she's upset about me letting Blaze watch or if this company is getting to her.

In my experience women can't deal with what I do for a living, but what she doesn't understand is I'm to a point now that I could walk away from that aspect of the business at any time. My guys will easily make enough money to keep it all going.

Besides that, I've invested my money like crazy and could easily work something else out if that's what's bothering her.

I can't fix something I don't know about though, so her not

talking to me is going to make me irritated.

Walking through the front room, I catch Levi standing at the bar. "I'll be back in a few. Make sure the ladies here to help get this place ready for tonight know what we need done."

It takes me only a few minutes to pull into the parking lot. I walk in knowing I'll be out of place, but I'm sure one of the clerks can help me.

"Hi, sir. Can I help you with something?" The hot blonde rushes to help me just as I enter the door.

"I need a sexy red dress that could also work at a black tie affair." I don't tell her the real kind of affair it'll be at, because it's really the same as far as the dress goes.

"I have a couple back here, follow me." I see in her eyes that she's disappointed I'm here shopping for a woman, but it is what it is.

"This one is backless and also low in the front, the material is great for a woman with nice curves because it tends to hug the body closely."

"That's the one."

"What size?" I have no idea what size she is, but quickly look to the blonde's body to compare.

"She has bigger tits than you and her ass is the perfect size, but she's about your height and size otherwise." She smiles and reaches for another hanger on the rack.

"This will be the one then. What about shoes?" Shit, I have no idea what size.

"Yes, red with sexy straps and all. Just give me the average size and the two sizes around it. I'll play it safe on those." She moves to pull some boxes down and hands them to me before she walks back to the counter.

"Anything else for you today? We have very sexy undergarments over there." She smiles and looks up at me once she gets the total.

"She won't be wearing any of those, but yes, I want your card. I may have you come and measure her so that I know exactly what size she is and can just call you when I need something." Her smile grows even larger and I realize this connection is something I need. It's a good thing to have for the business as well. There are many times we try to send a gift to one of the ladies for whatever reason and a place like this may be perfect for just that.

"Here you go!" I pay the ticket and take the dress and shoes from her, knowing I'm headed for Rebel's to convince her that she will be coming tonight. I just hope she likes the dress I chose.

I pull into her driveway and notice her Jeep parked in front of the garage door. I check my phone once more to see if she's messaged me only to confirm she hasn't.

She's ignoring my texts and it's time I teach her a fucking lesson.

Stepping out of my truck, I pull the dress from the passenger seat and lift the sack full of shoes. I see the curtain move before I get to her door, so I know she knows I'm here.

Before I have the chance to knock, the door flies open.

"What are you doing here?" She looks like she's been sleeping since she left my house.

"You won't answer my damn texts, so I'm here to tell you in person." Her eyes fall to the red dress before she looks at me confused. "There's a house party tonight. I want you there. It's formal, so I bought you a dress."

"You really shouldn't have, Lynx. I can't . . ." I stop her before she continues.

"You will be there. Here are some shoes as well. It starts at eight. I expect to see you there." She looks at me like she's surprised by my demand.

I extend the dress and shoes to her and then pull her against me. "I need to see you tonight. It's important to me." She has to know that I want to spend my nights with her by now.

She slowly lowers her head as I lean forward to kiss her, causing my lips to land on her forehead. Not being satisfied with that, I grip her face and bring her lips to mine to kiss her before I try to talk to her.

"What's going on in that gorgeous head of yours?" I have to know why she's changed so much since I took her to bed with me.

She swallows before she looks up at me. "I'm just really tired. I'll do my best to be there by eight." I decide to let her off easy, knowing she just finally agreed to come to my house tonight. If I need to talk to her more, I can then.

I lean forward once more to kiss her and this time she meets my lips perfectly. Pulling her body closer to mine, I kiss her deeper until we're both pulling away from the kiss. I wrap her in my arms and find myself inhaling her hair as I hold her.

It's like she's making me a crazy person and I need to pull back and give her some space. I'm not sure she's ready for what all of this means.

Chapter Twenty Six

Rebel

I TURN TO LOOK AT myself in the mirror from every angle. This dress is ridiculous and I may as well be wearing the paint again because it literally shows everything.

Lynx has my emotions running wild today and I'm not sure it's even a good idea that I go tonight. Seeing him with some of his callers may be the last straw for me when it comes to all of this.

Since meeting him, I've changed so much. I honestly don't even know who I am anymore. The things he has me wanting and thinking about shock me and I can't even imagine telling Remi about them, which should say a lot.

He pulls at me so much and I've been caught in his clutches since the first time I saw him.

I hear the door open and look to see Remi watching me. "Holy shit, Rebel. That is the sexiest I've ever seen you." Her mouth is wide open and if I'm not mistaken she looks like she's about to tear up.

"Thank you," I say, while watching her take me in.

"Are you off to a date again?" She walks closer, never taking her eyes away from the dress as she pulls on the material around my hips.

"Wow! I can't get over this. It's like it was literally made for you. Was it?"

"I don't think so." Her eyes catch the three boxes of shoes on my bed.

"He bought you all of these too?" I open one of the boxes to show her.

"They're all the same, just different sizes." She grabs the size nine and tucks it under her arm.

"This is the first day I'm excited that we don't wear the same size. Tell him I said thanks for the size nines." I laugh at her as I pull one of them out to look at closer.

"These are 'fuck me' heels. You know this right?" I let the long strap run through my fingers before I look over at her.

"I know. I wouldn't expect anything different from Lynx." She flops down on my bed before she begins to drill me.

"You don't even have a bra and panties on, do you?" I don't even have to answer, because she can see.

Everyone will be able to.

"Tell me he's as good as I imagine. I can't believe you are just so calm about all of this. You are literally fucking the one guy that hundreds . . . no wait . . . thousands want to fuck."

"Don't remind me." I move to the bathroom to finish my hair and makeup, trying to push that thought from my mind.

"Just remember, he's buying *you* stuff. That means he likes you. I mean, you got *the date*. How many do you think get that from a guy like him?"

"Honestly, I'm not sure."

"Is my Rebel falling for the bad boy? Because I feel like

there's something crazy brewing in that head of yours." I don't look at her because she'll be able to see through anything I say. She always does.

"I don't know what's going on between us. I can tell you he's a lot of fun and there's never a dull moment." *And I can feel myself falling for him.*

"I can only imagine how entertaining he is. Did you tell Rome about me yet? It's time you let your best friend in this house meet Rome." I turn to see how serious she is.

"I'll take you to work with me one of these days, then you can meet them all." She jumps up from my bed with a new boost of energy.

"Perfect. I'll go shopping for something to wear tonight!" She moves in to give my hair a few flips before she grabs the curling iron from me and curls a couple of strands in the back. "I'm guessing I'll see you tomorrow with the way you're dressed." We look at each other in the mirror and both smile.

"Probably," I say with a bit of hope.

"Just have fun and leave all the heavy shit at home. I promise it's just easier that way." She turns me around to wrap her arms around me before she leaves me to myself.

"Fun isn't the issue." I start talking to myself until I finish my makeup. "Everything's heavy with him."

The heels make my legs look great. I love how the strap wraps around my ankle and lower leg a few times. It's the sexiest pair of shoes I've owned in my entire life.

I decide to drive myself tonight so I have an out if I need one. The last house party had women coming out of the woodwork, so I can only imagine this will be the same.

Pulling up to the gate, I get an immediate pass and notice the attendant pick up the phone once I drive by. I look down at the clock and see that it's already nine o'clock, so I'm late. There are cars everywhere and my stomach begins to hurt knowing the house is even more packed than it was last time.

I park next to his garage on the backside of the house. There aren't any other cars back here and it gives me the space to leave if I choose to.

I'm stepping out of my Jeep when I see him walking toward me in the darkness. When he hits the part of the yard that's lit I can see that he's wearing a suit. *Damn, he looks extremely sexy tonight.*

"Fuck, Rebel. That dress was made for you." He pulls me in close the second he gets near me, as if he's been going crazy to touch me all night.

"Thank you for the dress." He moves my chin up slowly until I'm looking at his face.

"It's the first of many if I have it my way." He slowly kisses me and I take a deep breath, inhaling the night air around us. He pulls away to look at me.

"The house is packed." He puts his hand on the small of my back, touching bare skin as he runs the other hand over my chest and down my cleavage to pull it down just a little, exposing me to him. "I fucking love this dress on you."

It has no back and actually shows the top of my ass if I move just right. Of course it shows my cleavage and nearly half of my tits now that he's pulled it down lower, which is why he loves it.

We walk together until he opens the door to the house. I have to follow behind him once we get inside because there are so many people crowded in.

Once we get to the main foyer, I hear Rome talking on a mic long before I see him. "Alright, I need all of the Alpha guys up here. It's after nine. Time to bring this party to the level of a true Alpha."

I release Lynx's hand only to have him grab my hand again.

"Aren't you going up there?"

"No. I'm staying with you." He leans into my ear so I can hear him.

"Where's the boss man? We need pictures for the website. Get him up here too." I can hear Blaze talking over the speakers now as Lynx pulls me closer to the guys.

"Here he is. Ladies. This is the man behind the idea of the Alphachat Empire. You can make sure to thank him for all of his genius ideas to bring us all together on nights like this." Rome takes the mic from Blaze to give Lynx the introduction.

He releases my hand when the guys all yell for him to go up there. He quickly steps in line with the rest of the guys.

"Alright men, it's time to show the ladies what it means to come to a black tie affair in the Alpha House." I watch them all rip off their suits like strippers while the women scream in excitement.

I get pushed aside as they all push forward to get to the guys, so I walk halfway up the staircase to watch them.

Lynx is last to remove his clothes. They've all removed everything except tight underwear and a small bowtie around their necks. My eyes scan the insanity in the room and I instantly wish I wouldn't have come tonight.

It's one thing to know he does what he does on camera, but it's entirely different watching him like this even though I can see him searching for me.

When his eyes finally find me, he smiles and moves forward, allowing a few more of his fans to run their hands down his abs.

I feel my face get heated as they all continue to touch him. I can't even swallow through the disgust I feel. I can't watch this.

Remembering he has a bar in his office, I go inside and close the door. I pull out the tequila and take three shots back to back before I have a chance to see that there's a woman sitting at his desk.

"You must have it bad. Which one?" Her voice sounds loud in the otherwise quiet room. I look at her completely see through dress and regret coming in here for the tequila.

"Sorry, I didn't see you in here. I'm just having a rough day." I step toward the door before her words stop me in my tracks.

"If you see Lynx, will you tell him Viv is waiting for him, just like he asked me to?" My skin erupts with fire and even though I want to jump over everything in my path to her, I hold back my words because she's not the one they should be thrown at.

Anger takes over my thoughts and I just want to get the hell out of here before I lose my shit on this practically naked woman. I should've known something like this would happen.

He isn't what I need in my life. I need someone who wants me and only me. He isn't capable of that with all of this constant temptation around him every single day.

"If I see him, I'll give him the message," I say through gritted teeth. Releasing a hard breath, I walk out and slam the door behind me, before I slam right into the chest of one of the guys.

I look up to see Blaze's eyes burning into mine.

"Slow down, Woman. What's the rush?" I can't answer him because I honestly want to scream from the top of my lungs about the whore behind this door.

I push away from him only to see Lynx looking up at me. He's working his way toward the stairs through all the women and that's when I lose my mind.

I reach out and grab Blaze's hand to pull him along with me. "Where's your room?" I ask with urgency, even though I can feel him pulling back.

He yanks my hand back toward him after only a couple of feet.

"What's wrong, Rebel? Did someone hurt you?" I get closer

and just go for it. Pulling his face toward mine, I begin kissing him like I'll die if I don't. It takes him a few seconds to put his hands on me, but he eventually does.

He pulls away from me after his tongue makes its way around my mouth a few times.

"You're trying to get me killed, aren't you?" He pushes down on his hard on just as he says it and I pull his hand again, not backing down.

"No, just trying to finish what we started the other day." I have a right to make Lynx watch me with another man if I have to see all of this with him. We aren't exclusive anyway, so I'm going to take Remi's advice and have fun. I can leave all the emotional shit at home and just enjoy this for what it's worth. And apparently, all it's worth is a great fuck.

"What the fuck are you doing?" Lynx moves in front of me, quickly stopping me again in my tracks.

"Finishing what you started. Figured it's ok to play since you instigated it." He glares at me through a fierce look and I almost pull away to walk the fuck out of this house where I can get my sanity back. How dare he look at me like this when he has a naked whore in his office waiting for him as we speak.

"Is that what you want?" He moves closer and I can feel Blaze try to release my hand, but I hold tighter, not letting him out of my grip.

"You're damned right I do." I never move my eyes from his as I make a point to show him I don't want anything more from him than he can give.

"Fuck me, Lynx. Watch Blaze fuck me. Then fuck me again." He lowers his eyes as I speak and I can see something move over him.

"We do it in my room and I call the shots," he grinds out.

I release Blaze's hand and move away from Lynx.

"Fine. Don't make me wait."

I can hear their footsteps behind me as I walk around the corner to Lynx's bedroom.

I slide the straps of my dress down my shoulders the second I walk into his room. It's best if I just do this quick. My nerves may sneak through the tequila and anger if I wait another second.

Blaze closes the door before he turns to look at the dress around my feet before his eyes travel all the way up my body.

Lynx is already watching my face like he's trying to read me. *Read this.*

I walk over to Blaze and put my arms around his neck until he lowers his lips to mine.

He's even slower to put his hands on me this time. I reach around him and let my hands move over his firm ass. This damn underwear doesn't even cover their ass cheeks and I've been so distracted with being pissed off, I didn't even catch that minor detail.

I can feel Lynx behind me, slowly joining in. His touch feels warmer than Blaze's. He presses himself against me as he pulls my hips into his, grinding just slightly until I stop kissing Blaze.

Why does he get to make me feel like this? I tried like hell to avoid getting wrapped up in a situation just like this and now here I am. Tonight has to be the last time I step foot in his house or club.

Lynx consumes me and now all I'm trying to do is find a breath in the chaos he's caused in my life.

Damn him for making me like him when he's not really available.

Chapter Twenty Seven

Lynx

HOW THE HELL DID WE get to this?

"This is all for her. Hold back, because I swear I'll kill you if you come." Blaze nods at me as we follow her down the hall. I can tell he's not too sure about what he's been dragged into. Not that he's against a threesome; in fact, I know he's done this many times before. I'm sure he's just feeling my internal rage about her wanting this.

She slides her dress down her body and her long hair drapes over her shoulders and down her back. Her confidence in this situation surprises me, but I can tell she's changing with each time she's with me. She's getting more comfortable, obviously.

Knowing that Blaze is going to get to really see her during all of this makes me crazy, let alone when he actually gets the chance to touch her. I dig deep trying to remind myself that this is not his fault.

She moves for Blaze first and my heart sinks. Seeing her kiss him like this makes me want to yank her out of his arms and either beat the shit out of him or take it out on her by pounding that sweet pussy to remind her that she's mine.

Mine. That's not something I've thought about a woman before. What the fuck is wrong with me lately?

I move closer to her and try to process what's going on in my head. Her skin is soft. She's moving against him like she normally moves when we're together and it's bothering me.

She's aggressively kissing him while he's holding back. Fuck, she looks like she's about to climb him and mount his dick at this point.

I guess if she wants a threesome, it's time to let her have one. I've never dreaded sex like I do right now.

I pull her hips against my cock and get some friction to get me started. It only takes a few small thrusts against her before I begin to spring to life. I place my hands over her tits before I slide one down her body. She stops kissing him just as I do this.

"If this is what you want, we're going to give it to you, but you'd better make damn sure you're ready for me to be in that ass because that's where this is headed." She leans her body against mine and sways her ass a few times, sliding it over my cock while she moans out a sound of acceptance.

"If you want two men, you're getting us both at the same time."

Blaze smirks and I know he's ok with this and as far as he's concerned shit is about to go down. Any other day with any other woman I'd be excited, but this is Rebel. I swallow my emotions and give Blaze a nod, allowing him the permission he's waiting for.

I think this is going to be a true test to my patience and I hope like hell we all come out of this without any complicated emotions to follow.

Rebel

HE WANTS MY ASS? HIS dick is huge and he wants my ass. I've seen Blaze's and it's giant too, so this is going to be crazy. I hope I can take what they're about to give me.

I hate how I feel right now. This is turning me into the crazy person I was after Robert.

Blaze finally starts to touch me more after a few minutes even though Lynx's hands are everywhere. He's burning me with his touch even from behind while I work hard to focus on Blaze. Damn Lynx for the way he can get to me with such little effort.

Blaze is very attractive. His sexy scruff and blue eyes compliment that ridiculously sexy smile he has on his face at all times. Well, except right now. He's not smiling. I can see his demeanor changing as this progresses.

I reach down to feel the bulge in his underwear and can tell he's at least into me somewhat by the hardness of it.

I feel Lynx press down on my shoulder like he's sending me to my knees, so I lower Blaze's underwear on the way down. Lynx steps beside him quickly so I slide his down as well.

This is a lot of cock in my face. I try not to think about all of it fitting when it comes time for that. They're both pierced, so it'll be even more complicated.

I hold each one of them in my hands and inspect the metal. How can two dicks be so sexy? I usually don't consider penis to be attractive, but with these two it's like they were both blessed in this area.

Sliding my hands up and down each one of them, I look into Lynx's eyes. His dark eyes look over me and I'm not sure what I feel from his stare. I can't believe I let myself think a relationship with him would work in the slightest. The woman in his office is probably one of many that he's had in here since he started spending time with me. It's how men are. I've seen it enough times with the guys at Robert's tattoo shop.

Lynx wraps his hand in my hair and moves me forward until I open my mouth. He slides in slow, making sure to go as deep as he can until I pull back, gagging.

His tight grip in my hair allows him to pull me toward him again, going just as deep before he holds my head in place and adds even more pressure to the back of my throat. I can feel his piercing back there and it's making it even harder not to gag.

He finally releases my hair and I use my tongue a few times, which seems to calm the energy around Lynx. I wonder if the whore in his office will do this better for him?

Who am I calling a whore, when I'm down on my knees with two men in my hands? Well I guess if it's whores he likes, then he should love this because I plan to make this experience everything it's meant to be.

I take Lynx in my hand and move to bring Blaze's cock near my mouth. Jesus, this guy has to be a little wider than Lynx, but the length is close.

Before I have any more time to analyze it, Lynx is pulling my head back to him. He loves wrapping my hair into his fist and guiding me around when I'm on my knees and I'm not sure I want him to right now.

I never take my hand off of Blaze while Lynx begins to fuck my mouth again. He's relentless and not letting up even when I start to choke on him with every thrust.

"You want to suck dick. Then this. Is the dick. You will suck." His words sound angry, but I don't care. He can't be jealous after the shit I just saw in this house.

I pull my head back and look up at him. My stare is challenging and he matches me with emotion.

"Get up. You're not sucking his dick." I can see in his eyes that he means business. He's struggling with this arrangement and that's exactly what I hoped would happen.

I stand between them both and wait for someone to move. They both stand and wait, so I move for the bed. I'm not going to let Lynx dictate what happens here, so I sit against the head board and slide my hand between my legs.

I can't look at either of them, so I close my eyes and insert one finger, before I replace it with two. I begin to move my hips slightly before a boldness washes over me.

"Isn't this what you like? You like people watching. Maybe I should start doing this on camera." I grip my nipple with my other hand and slide my fingers into my mouth, tasting myself for the first time.

"Oh fuck." Blaze exhales just before he begins to stroke his cock. I grab my tits and play with my nipples a few times before I begin finger fucking myself again. I still haven't looked at Lynx, even though it's the heat from his stare that's getting to me.

"I can't take much more of this." Lynx barks at me as he grabs a condom and begins to slide it on, never turning his eyes from me.

"Rebel. Get your ass over here." I finally look into his eyes again. This time he's hungry. This time he's hiding whatever anger and jealousy he has and he looks like he's about to fuck me into tomorrow.

I crawl to him slowly, purposely making him wait on me. I'm on all fours, facing him when I get to the edge of the bed, and I know that tequila has encouraged half of this shit, but I don't care.

He slides a neck tie from his night stand and begins to tie it around my neck, leaving it hanging down my cleavage.

"Turn around." I listen only because he's leading me toward getting this over with. I want to do this so I can walk away from him forever. If he can watch me be with another man, then I'll know we aren't on the same page with this little relationship we've started.

He grips my hips and pulls me to the edge of the bed before he slams into me. "You want to be fucked hard, then I'm the one who'll do it." I almost scream from the intrusion, but hold it back. His piercing pounds against my insides with every thrust and I can't contain the rush of sexual emotions that he's bringing to surface.

He fucks me hard, over and over until I do scream out, even though I'm doing what I can to crawl away from his grip.

I don't want him that deep. I don't want him to make me scream. I want him to not affect me like he does but damn it, he gets to me.

"Feel my dick Rebel and remember it, because I'm walking the fuck out of this room. I won't watch you take another guy's dick like you do mine." He gives me one more deep thrust before he pulls out and leaves me there on the bed while he puts on a pair of jeans.

"You have my permission to do anything she wants. I'll be in my office." His words anger me and I crawl my way to Blaze before he walks out the door. I'm holding him in my hand as I try to make myself do this.

It isn't until I hear the door slam that the tears begin to build up in my eyes.

Blaze stands quietly while I just stare at his abs. He's not moving and neither am I.

"What are you doing, Rebel?" I can't answer him, because I don't know what I'm doing.

"Move over." He sits in the bed and pulls the covers over him before he leans against the head board. "Here, put this over you." I can see him pressing on his dick like he's trying to talk it down and I know he knows this is over.

"He can't walk away from seeing it when I don't have that choice. It's everywhere and I just don't think I can deal with that on a daily basis." I cover myself with the blanket and look at Blaze. His face is flustered and he's trying to listen to what I have to say.

The poor guy has been dragged into this and now he has to listen to me rant.

"I think you two need to talk."

"I can't ask him to not do the job that makes him all this money. That's not fair of me." He doesn't say anything else when I stand to put my dress on. In fact, he doesn't watch me put it on like I figured he would. I guess I'm not his type.

"Sorry if I inconvenienced you in all this. I'm sure I'm not your type anyway." He stands and holds the blanket against his cock.

"You aren't my type, because you and I both know you're taken. I don't do that to my friends. Lynx has it bad for you and I respect that. But if it wasn't for that, I promise you I would be fucking you right this very second. That's why I'm standing here holding my dick trying to get my shit together before I leave this room." His words leave us both awkward and I'm ok with that, knowing I probably will never see him again.

"Thanks for that. Can you help me get out the back door? I can't walk by his office with that whore in there." He pulls up his underwear and adjusts himself into place as he begins talking.

"Wait a minute, what whore are you talking about?"

"The one in his office." I stop talking and decide that I need to really be done with this night before I do even more shit that

I'll regret tomorrow. "Can we not talk about it and just get me out of here?" I don't want to rehash how I'm not enough for Lynx and he needs to have someone waiting on standby when I'm around.

"Yeah. Let me make myself presentable here because I'm driving you home." He puts on a pair of Lynx's shorts and throws the blanket back on the bed before we both leave the room. I want to tell him I'll drive myself, but the truth is I know I've had too much to drink.

He takes me down a set of stairs in the back that I didn't even know about that end in Lynx's garage. He makes a call, asking for my address to tell someone to meet him in a few minutes. Then he reaches for my keys and tells me to get in.

The drive to my house is completely silent and I guess you could call it the drive of shame before I make the *walk of shame* into my house once he drops me off.

Blaze stands there as I open the door and walk away from everything that is Lynx Kade.

I guess I didn't do so well at just having fun and leaving my emotions at home.

Chapter Twenty Eight

Lynx

IT'S BEEN THREE FUCKING DAYS since I've heard from Rebel and it isn't for lack of trying. Every time things calm down enough around the house, I call her or text her, just to have her ignore my ass.

I tried to give her what she wanted, but I just couldn't do it. The thought of watching Blaze drive his cock into her, had my blood boiling and my head about ready to fucking explode with rage.

I'll give her anything she wants, *except* for that. That is the one thing I can't do when it comes to Rebel. I'll fucking die before sharing her with another man and watching her face heat up with pleasure from someone else other than me.

When I went back to my office that night, I was surprised to see Viv in my office waiting for me. Yeah, I asked her to meet me there for a business meeting, but that was the last thing on my mind after the shit that went down with Blaze.

I invited Viv in the hopes of getting insight into hopefully bringing a female into business at the Alpha House and broaden our audience a bit. Some of the women that browse our website send emails asking if there will ever be any females available.

I'm considering the possibility, but nothing is set in stone.

My head just wasn't into business that night, so I sent her down to the party and I retired to my bedroom to get my thoughts in check.

It was a long fucking night.

Blaze has been giving me awkward looks all fucking day and I catch him looking at me as if he's trying to tell me some shit without saying it.

"Things are good between us, Blaze. You can stop acting so fucking weird now. I don't hate you for fucking Rebel."

He takes a seat on the stool next to mine and calls Envy over to order us a few shots of whiskey. "What kind of asshole do you take me for? *I didn't fuck her.* I took her home because she reeked of fucking tequila then had Envy bring me back to the house." He tosses his shot back at the same time I do.

"You dick. I've been miserable thinking about you fucking what's mine." He starts to laugh as he signals for another round of shots for us.

"Rebel's gotten to you, Lynx. You haven't been the same since you walked out that fucking door and I bet she hasn't been either."

I look down at my phone when it buzzes in my hand, but throw it across the bar when I see it's not Rebel. He's one hundred percent right, I haven't been the same. "I don't know what to fucking do. She won't return any of my calls or texts. Something was wrong with her that night and that shit she pulled was completely out of character for her. Even if she liked the thought of someone watching I can't believe she's the two dick type. I can't fix that shit if I don't know what was going on with her. Fuck!"

Blaze narrows his eyes at me. "You seriously don't know how much your career hurts her, do you? Or the fact that you had a woman waiting in your office for you that night?" He lets out a laugh of disbelief as I watch him. "Rebel is different. She's not the kind of woman that's just going to be okay with that kind of stuff."

"Fuck." I slam my fist down onto the bar, when I realize that she must've seen Viv in my office and got the wrong impression. "It was about business, Blaze. I didn't call Viv over to *fuck*. I wouldn't do that to Rebel."

"Well, Rebel doesn't know that. As far as she knows, you had a *whore* in your office. That's where you disappeared to after leaving her alone with me so . . . ."

I squeeze my eyes shut and feel my chest tighten. No wonder she was pushing so damn hard for a threesome with Blaze. I hoped with everything in me it wasn't because she wanted him.

"It's hard for her to see how many women get to watch you jerk your shit. She *does* do all of the scheduling so she sees it all. She cares about you. She really fucking cares about you. I could see it in her eyes that night." He tosses back another shot. "Hell . . . I might even say she's falling for your ass."

My chest aches with a need I've never felt when he talks about her feelings. Hell, I've never cared how a woman felt before Rebel.

"I don't know." I toss back my second shot of whiskey and look out to watch the people on the dance floor. I came here to check on the club and give my mind something to do, but I ended up tossing back drinks to clear my head instead. "She's too good. She's perfect and I'm far from it."

Blaze laughs. "I won't argue that."

I give him a hard look, before looking back out at all of the people dancing.

"Maybe she's not looking for perfect or hell . . . maybe she sees perfect when she looks at you. Perfect for her and that's all that really matters to a woman. A good one anyway. Just give her a few more days. If she doesn't come to you, take your ass to her and give her no choice."

"That's what I plan to do." I shake my head. "I don't know if I can give her a few more days."

Blaze smiles. "That says a lot. So what are you gonna do? Quit taking calls?"

"Yeah," I say quickly.

Blaze's eyes widen. "Are you serious?"

"Dead serious."

"Ok . . . then who will take the top spot? It's always been you. That might lose the site a lot of business."

"I don't care if it does. You boys bring in enough business to keep things rolling." I stop and take a swig of my beer. "You," I say, answering his first question.

He spits his drink out over his lap. "Fuck! Are you serious about that shit?"

I nod my head and slap his shoulder. "Yeah. You deserve the spot and the extra pay. You're top Alpha now. Get used to it and don't fuck up."

"Oh fuck. I won't." He sits up straighter and practically breaks his neck to follow some chick in the crowd of dancing bodies. "She's here."

"Who?" I follow his eyes to see Karma in the crowd, dancing without a care in the world. She looks completely lost in the song, her hands running over her sweaty body with her eyes closed.

"Talk later, Boss."

I laugh to myself as Blaze rushes across the room and slides his body in between Karma and some guy that was getting close to her.

"Do you need another one, Boss?"

I turn around to face Envy and toss down a fifty. She's been eyeing me with heated eyes ever since she finally saw me for the first time. Before the other night, Brit was the only one of my bartenders that knew what I looked like. I hired her in the beginning.

She brushes her hand up my arm and pulls her bottom lip between her teeth. "Anything at all I can do for you?"

"Keep your fucking hands to yourself," I say in reply to her question. "And follow the fucking rules. I'll be in my office." I feel her eyes on me as I stand up and walk away, but the last thing I am is turned on.

Rebel is still the only woman that I want to be with and that tells me I'm doing exactly what I should be doing.

Tomorrow I am going in and pulling my name down from the website and moving Blaze up in my spot.

Then I'm going to fight like hell to give Rebel a few more days, before I end up at her door, uninvited. And I won't be leaving until I get what I want.

Her...

Rebel

IT'S BEEN FIVE DAYS SINCE I've seen Lynx and two days since I've heard from him. Maybe he finally got the hint that I want nothing to do with him. Maybe he finally sees that I just can't handle being hurt by him. His lifestyle is far from what I can take.

I thought using Blaze would make everything better and make me somewhat ok with what he does, but it did *nothing* to ease the pain that I feel when I think about him and other women.

He had a practically naked woman waiting for him in his office for crying out loud. And he didn't even act as if it was a big deal. *He* left me there with Blaze while he went to *her.*

Who just does that? He could've at least had the decency to go to another room, other than where some woman was waiting to fuck him.

Every time I replay the events of that night in my head, it hurts a little more each time. It's slowly killing me inside and making it hard for me to focus on anything but.

"Whatcha doing?" Remi walks into my room, taking a seat on the end of my bed. She's been on my ass since that night. "You still working? You've been working nonstop for almost four days now. Stop."

I shake my head and squeeze my eyes shut, to ease the pain from staring at the computer. "No. I can't. I need to make up for the money I won't be making from the Alpha House or club now. You'll see me in about a week when I'm all caught up. I'm fine. I'm a big girl."

"No," she says firmly. "You're far from fine and I don't like it. I want my best friend back, dammit."

Ignoring her, I fight back the lump in my throat and focus on the website I'm designing for one of my clients. Right now, that's what's important. "It is what it is, Remi."

She goes quiet for a few seconds, making me believe that she might actually just leave me alone finally. "Have you heard from Lynx since the other day?"

Nope. I obviously hoped for too much.

"Remi- let's not get into this right now. Please. I can't . . ."

"Just stop for two damn seconds and talk to me," she snaps.

Hearing her sound so angry snaps me out of the daze I've

been in for the last few days. "I'm sorry. It's just hard to talk about. I want to tell you but . . ."

"But what?" she pushes.

"It hurts too much," I admit. "My heart feels like it's been ripped from my chest and stomped on. It's hard to breathe. It's hard to think. It's hard to do a lot of things. I feel like I took a trip back to my past and that's something I swore I'd never do again." I stop and release a breath. "But the worst part of it all . . . I miss him and the way he made me feel when we were together."

"Oh, Honey." She stands up and walks over to wrap her arms around my neck. "Maybe you should just talk to him."

I rest my head against hers for a second, before pulling away and wiping at my face. "It doesn't matter if I talk to him. It won't change a thing and I'm not willing to force a change in his life. He's worked hard to get where he is and the last thing he needs is some chick ruining it all for him. I won't be *that* girl."

"Maybe he wants you to be *that* girl. Maybe he wants to hear how much it's hurting you so he can fix it. You can't expect a problem to be fixed if the person causing it doesn't even know it's a problem. Have you even told him how you feel?"

I shake my head as she backs away and sits on my desk. "It doesn't matter. He invited me to a party, yet he had one of his *callers* there waiting for him in his office. A man like that doesn't want to hear how I feel about him."

Remi narrows her eyes at me. "How do you know she was there for the reason you're thinking? Men are stupid, but I don't see Lynx being *that* stupid. Especially after he worked hard to get you there in the first place. Maybe you need to stop being a pussy and confront him."

"Really!" I laugh a little as she smiles down at me. "I'm not being a pussy. I'm just trying to save the heartache."

"You are being a pussy. And if it's enough to cause heartache then maybe it's worth it. I haven't seen you this way over a guy . . . well, ever. It didn't even effect you this much when Robert cheated on you and you were with him for almost two years. That's a hell of a lot longer than you've known Lynx. But . . ." she pauses and plays with my hair. "Sometimes it only takes a few weeks."

Closing my eyes, I take a deep breath and let her words sink in. Maybe she's right. Lynx is worth so much more than what I've been trying to let on since that night. He's crawled his way so deep under my skin that he's the first and last thing that I think about every damn day.

"I'll think about talking to him. I just need a little more time to get my thoughts in check so I don't say the wrong thing. You know how I get when I'm upset. Things don't come out right and my emotions are just running high right now." I know if I don't at least agree to think about talking to him, she'll never leave me alone about this.

"Oh, I know more than anyone and I don't want that either."

With that, she kisses me on the top of the head and leaves me alone. She'll most likely be watching Jason Statham movies for the rest of the night, so I know she'll leave me alone to work now.

Except, my mind's on Lynx even more now than ever.

The only way to get him off of it is to work even harder to forget him. I'll just have to dive even deeper into my work because I can't expose myself to that kind of life again.

I just hope that it doesn't kill me in the process . . .

Chapter Twenty Nine

Lynx

FUCK! I THOUGHT THE ACHE in my chest would fade after being away from Rebel for more time. I was completely wrong. The longer I'm away from her, the more my chest feels as if it's going to burst the fuck open.

It has nothing to do with the fact that I've been doing the admin work and drowning myself in the chaos of the business. I could care less. It wasn't her making things easier on me that made me want her here. And it definitely wasn't just her body that kept me craving her.

It was so much more and I see that now.

Her smile. Her laugh. Her fucking eyes. The way she would look at me from across the room or challenge me. It all made me feel more alive than I have in years.

Ripping the check from the book, I shove it in an envelope and address it to Rebel. I don't know why the fuck I added her address. Maybe to make it look like I sent it instead of hand delivered it.

She might not want anything to do with me at the moment, but that doesn't change the fact that I want to take care of her. I offered her a year contract and that's exactly what I plan to pay her for.

I owe her so much more than that. She's given me something I never thought I'd have: an ache to love a woman and to be loved.

I'd give it all up if it meant I'd get to wake up next to her every morning. That one night she slept here with me was a fucking tease. Something to torture me and remind me of what I don't have.

It could be love. It might not be. All I know is that it's driving me fucking crazy and fucking with my head.

Standing up from my desk, I grab my jacket and tell the guys that I'll be gone for most of the day. I need to be alone so I can figure out how this is all going to go down.

I drive around on my motorcycle for most of the afternoon. I forget about the Alpha House, the club and anything business related and think about just what I'm willing to do to prove to Rebel that I'm worth her time.

I'm not the flowers and candy sort of guy, but fuck . . . I'd be that for her if that's what I knew she wanted.

She's not that kind of girl, but maybe that's because nobody has ever done those things for her.

Taking a deep breath, I jump back on my bike and head to the diner where I know her roommate works. I need to make sure that Remi checks the mailbox when she gets off work.

Opening the door, she's the first person that I spot. She's leaning over the counter.

Her eyes land on mine as she looks my way and I can tell with that small glance that she knows why I'm here.

She almost looks hopeful to see me.

"Lynx," she greets me. "I'm guessing you're not here to eat since I've never seen you in here before."

I smile and shake my head. "You're right. I'm not. I need you to do me a favor."

She looks at me for a few seconds as if she's trying to read my intentions to see if they're genuine. Then her face turns into the biggest smile I've ever fucking seen.

"Take a seat. I'm off in five."

Fuck . . . I need this to work. I have a feeling this might be the push I need to get her out of the house and confront me.

༄

Rebel

I'VE BEEN STARING AT MY phone for the last hour, trying to find the courage to call Lynx and ask him to meet me so we can talk.

I don't want to step foot in the Alpha House. It's too soon for that and will only remind me of what could've possibly gone down at the party after I left.

I look up when Remi rushes inside, tossing her keys down onto the couch. "Have you left the computer at all today? Please tell me you have."

Rolling my eyes at the way she's looking at me with judgmental eyes, I shut down my computer and turn to face her. "I'm just now getting done with work. It's only five. I'm getting better."

"Good. Some mail came for you." She reaches her hand out with a grin. "Looks pretty important."

My heart instantly starts hammering when I see it came from the Alpha House. "This wasn't in the mailbox when I checked it earlier."

"Well . . . it was there now. Just open it."

Wanting some privacy, I push away from the computer and walk past Remi, to my room. Which doesn't really help since she comes over to stand in my doorway anyway, watching me like a hawk.

Taking a calming breath, I open the envelope and pull out a check that is written out to me for a ridiculous amount of money. "Holy shit!" I throw my hand over my mouth and fight to catch my breath. "Is he fucking insane?"

Remi rushes into my room and snatches the check out of my hand. "Holy fucking shit! There's a lot of zeros on this check." She starts fanning herself off. "I can't breathe. I've never seen so much money in my life."

"Doesn't matter," I say in anger, while snatching it from her hand and ripping it in half. "I'm not accepting it."

Remi watches me as I reach for my jacket and keys. "Where are you going?"

"To throw this at his face for even thinking I'd accept this. He doesn't owe me anything."

My heart is pounding so hard and fast that I can't make out what Remi is saying from behind me as I storm through the living room and yank the door open.

My whole world stops and heat spreads throughout my whole body as I look up to see Lynx standing in front of me in a pair of dress slacks, a black button down shirt and a loose tie.

He slowly looks up at me and holds up a single daisy. My mother used to always buy me daisies when I was sick as a child. They always made me feel safe because they were the flowers that my parents had at their wedding and every single anniversary party.

My breath hitches in my throat as he reaches out with his

free hand and grabs my chin. "I see you got my check."

I close my eyes and swallow, trying my hardest to not melt into him right now. "I did," I whisper. "And I don't want it. Here." I shove it into his chest, but instead of grabbing it, he lets it fall to the ground at our feet as he yanks me to him and crushes his lips against mine, so hard that it knocks my breath right out of me.

"We need to talk," I say between kisses.

His grip on my arms steadies me and I take in his kiss because I've missed it so much. He lifts my legs around his waist and carries me outside while he continues to kiss me.

"I've missed you like crazy and I can't stop thinking about you." He stops kissing me just long enough to set me down and then pulls my lips to his again.

His kiss is desperate, just like mine. I let my hands run down his back before I push between us to break the kiss.

"I can't believe you think I'd take that check. I'll be just fine without your money, or that job." I have to step away from him. When he's this close, I can't think straight.

"Come for a drive with me." He grabs my hand in his and tries to lead me toward his truck.

"Lynx. I can't. I can't do all of this again." My words stop him and he bows his head before he steps against me again.

"Yes you can. I need to talk to you." He doesn't kiss me this time, even though he's within an inch of my face. His eyes burn into mine and I know I have to go with him. We need to have this talk even though I know what I have to do.

"Can I at least brush my hair?" I look like hell and the fact that he's still rushing me actually surprises me even more when I think about what I'm wearing. "And change."

"Whatever you want to do. I have all the time in the world." He smiles at me when he says that and I can't help but catch a different look in his eyes.

"I'll be right out." I walk slowly through the house trying to wrap my head around what I'm going to say to him.

Remi isn't around to quiz me or harass me even though I know she's in the house. I think she knows I need this moment.

I exhale when I catch a glimpse in the mirror at my hair. "Really Rebel? You look like shit." Talking to myself, I rush to put my hair up. It's really the only saving grace I have at this point. I'll just get this conversation over and then I can lock myself back up in this room.

I smooth out my clothes and take a deep breath before I go back outside to meet him. He's still standing against the truck and smiling when he moves to open the door for me.

"Where are we going?" I have to ask even though my guess is he'll make me wait 'til he gets me there. In fact, the way he is, I'm sure he's just hauling me back to the Alpha House.

"You'll see. Put this on." He hands me a blindfold and I begin to shake my head no at him. He ignores me as he hands me my seatbelt.

"No, Lynx. We need to talk."

"I know, but not until I take this off of you. Just humor me." I hesitate before I give in and tie the blindfold around my head. I can hear him open his door and get in before he sits quiet.

I keep waiting for him to say something, but instead he starts the engine and we begin to move.

He's silent as we drive a few minutes and stop again. "Don't move. I'll come around and take you inside." My mind begins to wonder where he's taken me. I'm not worried, just curious. What I'm worried about is how I'm going to be able to stay away from him when he tries to talk to me with his body.

My heart rate picks up and I'm saddened as I realize the talk I'm about to have will end any future contact with this man, even though he makes me *feel*.

He opens the door and guides me out of the truck, being careful with me. "I'm going to carry you in, wrap your legs around me again." He smells so damn good. I can feel myself sliding back into my cravings having him this close again.

He carries me awhile and my heart sinks when I hear someone else close a door. "Almost there. I'm going to set you down and then we can talk." He slides the blindfold from my head and wraps his arms around me from behind as I begin to take in everything in sight.

"Where are we?" My mouth falls open at the size of the living room I'm staring at.

"My new house." I quickly turn around to face him before I start asking questions.

"What?"

"Rebel. You've changed me. I want to be with you and focus on a future with you. We can't do that in the Alpha House. I know that."

I step around him to see the massive kitchen and view of the gorgeous pool outside.

"I'm not taking calls anymore." His deep voice gets closer as he talks, until I can feel him right behind me again.

"What are you talking about, Lynx? You can't walk away from that kind of money." My heart is pounding faster with every word he says.

"I'm not. I still own the business and will have to work, but you'll be the only one to see my dick." This is all too much so I begin to walk around the bar in the kitchen to take a second.

"I can't ask you to do all of this," I say softly.

"You didn't. This is what I want. I want you, Rebel." He steps in front of me before I can get by him. "I know it's crazy, but you make me feel shit that I can't explain. I love how you make me feel and I need you in my life every single day. It's not fair for you to have to see what goes on in that house especially with that asshole in your past."

Wait . . . what?

He's quit taking calls? He bought a separate house? For me?

My head is spinning.

"I don't know what to say." He has me speechless and fighting for air.

"Don't say anything. Just let me take us back a few days and start again. I can promise you intensity and constant sex. I can promise you faithfulness and a place to stay every night, but I can't even imagine seeing you with another guy."

"Lynx, I didn't . . ." He interrupts me right away.

"I know. And neither did I. Vivian was a potential addition to the chat site, but I changed my mind about females. I forgot she was in my office when I left you with Blaze."

"She was wearing a see through dress."

"And it did nothing for me . . ." He slides his hands down my arms again. "Because it wasn't you. Don't you see, you've fucked me up in the best way possible. I look forward to being with you. Touching you. Kissing you. Fucking you. And one day making love to you. You're my every focus and I don't want anything to come between us."

I take in everything he's saying and can't help but feel relief wash over me. "I feel the same way. Do you know how miserable I've been the past few days?" My voice holds pain and I can see it in his eyes that he feels it too.

"I've heard."

Remi. It sounds just like her.

I step toward him and this time I'm the one that crashes into his body. My lips hit his and I lift my legs around his waist with desperation.

His arms take me in and he just stands in place as we

practically rip each other's clothes off, our mouths devouring every inch of each other that they can touch.

"I'm taking you to bed. My dick is about to explode. I'm not used to this dry spell shit."

I laugh as he starts to walk and I can feel my insides clench at the thought of him sliding inside me again.

Am I dreaming? Because if I am, I don't ever want to wake up.

Epilogue

Rebel

"I'VE MISSED YOU." HE PULLS me against his naked body, causing me to smile.

"I just made a pot of coffee."

"I know, it took forever." He shifts his hips against my ass and I feel his erection against my back.

"You're so impatient." I laugh softly.

"Hmmm. I am. What can I say, I could do this right here for the rest of my life."

I roll over and push him onto his back. We've been inseparable for nearly six weeks now and I can't complain in the slightest. He makes me happy and keeps me on my toes constantly.

Seriously, I couldn't ask for more right now.

I push his arms over his head as I climb onto him. Sliding his bare erection inside me, I start to move my hips slowly as I look into his eyes.

"God, I love you, Lynx. You make me feel." He thrusts his hips slowly, causing me to gasp as his piercing hits my G spot.

"You feel *that*, don't you?"

"Yessss." He grips my hips and moves me up and down slowly, each time bringing me closer to moaning through an orgasm.

"Ride me, baby." He puts his arms behind his head while I rotate my hips and take him in. "I love you too. Move in with me." I pause and he grinds into me again, gripping my hips tighter.

"I stay here every night," I say, out of breath.

It's true. Every single night since he brought me here, he's managed to get me to stay, not that he has to try anymore.

"But I want this to be your home. Right here in this bed, on my cock. Baby, call this home." He thrusts upwards, hitting me just right.

"It is home," I admit. "You are my home."

I feel complete. He makes me happy and I know there will never be a dull moment living with him. Moving in with him is an easy decision.

※

Lynx

THE WAY MY HEART FEELS when she says I'm her home is indescribable. There's never been a better feeling in the whole fucking world.

Pressing my lips to her neck, I reach one hand up to wrap into the bottom of her hair and I pull her down onto my dick as far down as she can go.

The way she grinds her hips into me and gasps has me extremely close to losing my shit already.

"Fuck, I love you so much." I run my tongue up her neck and dig my fingers into her hip as she rides me nice and slow. "You know the right way to work me. Keep moving like that, baby."

Her nails dig into my chest and abs, as she moves her hips a few more times, letting me bury myself as deep as I can go.

"I'm about to come," she pants above me. "Will you come with me, Lynx? I want to feel you inside of me."

"Well fuck . . ." Just hearing her say that she wants to feel me lose my shit inside of her has me over the edge, barely holding on. "Without the condom?"

"Yes." I've known she's on the pill for weeks now, but she always wants me to use a condom since I have the piercing. She's been worried about it healing correctly. Hell, so was I, but when it comes to fucking her I tend to forget all logic.

I grip onto her and begin to move my hips, grinding into her over and over again. "We're never using a fucking condom again, then. You know that, right?"

She nods her head and digs her nails deeper into me, drawing blood. "I'm coming. Oh, God . . ."

On her word, I push into her and stop, releasing myself as she clenches around me.

"Holy fuck!" With force, I pull her face down to mine and kiss her, before burying myself into her neck, while we both fight for air.

"Knock fucking knock."

Fucking Blaze.

"Are we too late?" Knox adds. "Did we miss it?"

Rebel laughs into my neck as their voices continue to talk right outside of our bedroom door.

"Wait in the bar, fuckers. Give us ten minutes."

Knox's head pokes around to look inside. "What was that, Boss? I can't hear . . ."

Rebel grabs for the nearest pillow and tosses it at Knox's head, stopping his words. "Go!"

The boys don't say anything else.

We smile at each other as we listen to their footsteps heading toward the bar.

"So much for privacy. What the fuck was the point of getting a separate house if I still have to see these dicks every day?"

Rebel smiles and watches me quickly dress. "You'll always

be the boss. Your guys aren't going anywhere. There's no escape," she teases.

Holy shit, she makes me so happy. And the fact that she accepts the boys just as I do, only makes her more perfect for me.

There's no way I'm letting her go. I just hope she can handle how much love I have to give her.

COMING SOON ~ Book 2 in the Alphachat.com Series

To receive a text on release day text 'PLAY' to 213-802-5257

Or sign up for both of the author's newsletters which can be found on their websites!

About the Authors

Victoria Ashley

VICTORIA ASHLEY GREW UP IN Rockford, IL and has had a passion for reading for as long as she can remember. After finding a reading app where it allowed readers to upload their own stories, she gave it a shot and writing became her passion.

She lives for a good romance book with tattooed bad boys that are just highly misunderstood and is not afraid to be caught crying during a good read. When she's not reading or writing about bad boys, you can find her watching her favorite shows such as Supernatural, Sons Of Anarchy and The Walking Dead.

She is the author of Wake Up Call, This Regret, Slade, Hemy, Cale, Stone, Get Off On The Pain, Something For The Pain, Thrust, Royal Savage and is currently working on more works for 2016.

Contact her at:
Website: *www.victoriaashleyauthor.com*
Facebook: *www.facebook.com/VictoriaAshleyAuthor*
Twitter: @VictoriaAauthor
Instagram: VictoriaAshley.Author

Books by
VICTORIA ASHLEY

WAKE UP CALL

THIS REGRET

SLADE (WALK OF SHAME #1)
HEMY (WALK OF SHAME #2)
CALE (WALK OF SHAME #3)

STONE (WALK OF SHAME 2ND GENERATION #1)

THRUST

GET OFF ON THE PAIN
SOMETHING FOR THE PAIN

ROYAL SAVAGE (SAVAGE & INK #1)

Hilary Storm

HILARY STORM LIVES WITH HER high school sweetheart and three children in Oklahoma. She drives her husband crazy talking about book characters everyday like they are real people. She graduated from Southwestern Oklahoma State University with an MBA in Accounting. Her passions include being a mom, writing, reading, photography, music, mocha coffee, and spending time with friends and family. She is a USA Today best-selling author of the Rebel Walking Series, Bryant Brother's Series, Inked Brother's Series, Six, and a co-author in the Elite Forces Series.

Contact her at:
Webpage: *www.hilarystormwrites.com*
Social Links
Facebook: *www.facebook.com/pages/Hilary-Storm-Author*
Twitter: @hilary_storm
Goodreads: *www.goodreads.com*

Books by
HILARY STORM

Six (Blade and Tori's story)
Seven (Coming in June)

Rebel Walking Series
In A Heartbeat
Heaven Sent
Banded Together
No Strings Attached
Hold Me Closer
Fighting the Odds
Never Say Goodbye
Whiskey Dreams

Inked Brothers Series
Jake One
Jake Two
Jake Three Coming Soon

Bryant Brothers Series
Don't Close Your Eyes

Elite Forces Series
ICE
FIRE

ACKNOWLEDGMENTS

Victoria Ashley

FIRST AND FOREMOST, I'D LIKE to say a HUGE thank you to Hilary Storm for taking a chance and writing this amazing story with me. It's my first time co-writing a book and I couldn't be more excited to have Hil with me on this journey. It's been quite a ride and I look forward to teaming up again to bring you some more sexy Alphas.

I'd also like to thank the beta readers that took the time to read Pay for Play: SE, Amy, Keeana, Lindsey and Amanda. We appreciate you ladies so much!

Kellie Montgomery for doing a wonderful job at editing and Dana Leah for her amazing design work on our cover.

And I want to say a big thank you to all of my loyal readers that have given me support over the last couple of years and have encouraged me to continue with my writing. Your words have all inspired me to do what I enjoy and love. Each and every one of you mean a lot to me and I wouldn't be where I am if it weren't for your support and kind words.

Last but not least, I'd like to thank all of the wonderful book bloggers that have taken the time to support our book and help spread the word. You all do so much for us authors and it is greatly appreciated. I have met so many friends on the way and you guys are never forgotten. You guys rock. Thank you!

ACKNOWLEDGMENTS

Hilary Storm

WOW WHAT A FUN RIDE this has been! I have to give a huge thanks to Victoria for wanting to write with me! I've always loved her writing and it was a great experience working alongside her for this book! Nothing like building from the heat we both already write on our own! V- thanks for being so patient with me during my tough personal times as this book was being written! It's been a great time and I can't wait until the next in the series!

My husband and kids are my life. Without their love and support I could never do any of this. It is through them that I have learned to love, live, and take chances. My heart is full because of these four and this book is no exception to that!

Steph . . . you always tell it to me just like it is and I appreciate you more than you'll ever know! Thanks for being my 12PIC!

Betas Amanda, Amy, Lindsey, Keeana, and Steph . . . thanks for taking time out of your life to help us perfect this bad boy!

Kellie- Thanks for cleaning it up for us! I love ya girl and I'm happy to have you in on this one!

Betas . . . I want to thank you all for pointing out the imperfections! We loved hearing from each of you and appreciate you taking the time to help make this possible!

Our loyal followers who will love this and share it like crazy, just like they always do. AND to the bloggers who support the author community . . . It is because of you that we keep writing with the urgency we do. We can't wait to share our stories with you so we can see how you react. Thank you for always allowing us to be a part of your lives through our words.

Printed in Great Britain
by Amazon